Josie tucked a strand of hair behind her ear. "Ready?"

He'd been so engaged in watching her that he hadn't done anything else. Art cleared his throat. "All right. Need a wrap?"

"Just a sweater, please."

Art reached behind the door for where she stored them. He ran his hand along the four or five there. "Which?"

"This one." Josie brushed past him and smiled as it slid from the hook into her arms. The fabric felt like a caress. Maybe they should stay in. . . . Another look at her face and her excitement and he decided no. They'd explore the amusement park first. She pulled on her sweater, her face inches from his. She must have read something in his expressions, because a softness claimed her.

"Later." Promise filled the single soft word she breathed. He nodded. He could wait.

He tore his eyes from her mouth and gestured toward the door. "This way, milady."

CARA C. PUTMAN lives in Indiana with her husband and three children. She's an attorney, lecturer at a Big Ten university, and a ministry leader and teacher at her church. She has loved reading and writing from a young age and now realizes it was all training for writing books. An honors graduate of the University of Nebraska and George Mason University School of Law, Cara loves bringing history to life. Her first book, *Canteen Dreams*, won the 2008 American Christian Fiction Writers Book of the Year in the short historical category. Cara regularly guest blogs at CRAFTIE Ladies of Suspense and at Writer Interrupted, as well as writing at her blog, The Law, Books & Life. To learn more about her other books and the stories behind the series, be sure to visit her at www.caraputman.com.

Books by Cara C. Putman

HEARTSONG PRESENTS
HP771—Canteen Dreams
HP799—Sandhill Dreams
HP819—Captive Dreams

Don't miss out on any of our super romances. Write to us at the following address for information on our newest releases and club information.

Heartsong Presents Readers' Service
PO Box 721
Uhrichsville, OH 44683

Or visit www.heartsongpresents.com

A Promise Kept

Cara C. Putman

Heartsong Presents

To my husband, Eric. We've walked through so much together, but I can't imagine traveling this road with anyone else. I love you.

Special thanks to Sue Lyzenga for reading this book for me literally as it scrolled off the printer. Your eagle eyes caught many errors. And to Tricia Goyer, Sabrina Butcher, and Gina Conroy for helping me fine tune the beginning.

A note from the Author:
I love to hear from my readers! You may correspond with me by writing:

Cara C. Putman
Author Relations
PO Box 721
Uhrichsville, OH 44683

ISBN 978-1-60260-503-9

A PROMISE KEPT

All scripture quotations are taken from the King James Version of the Bible.

Our mission is to publish and distribute inspirational products offering exceptional value and biblical encouragement to the masses.

PRINTED IN THE U.S.A.

The tick of the second hand rounding the face of the grand-father clock jarred the sudden silence in the small church anteroom. Josephine Miller stared at it, praying it could some-how speed up. Her wedding would start in a matter of minutes. The thought was wonderful. Why did time slow and each second seem to take a minute when all she wanted to do was sweep out of the room and race down the aisle?

In the middle of these crazy, uncertain times, Art Wilson had swept her off her feet and made her feel cherished in a way that blocked out everything.

She turned to look in the mirror standing against the wall; her fingers fidgeted with the pleats as she scanned her appearance. Her white gown flowed around her like a dress designed for a princess. Mama had managed to tame Josie's hair into a sleek upsweep, so different from how she looked most days. Her mother sighed, and Josie caught her gaze in the mirror's reflection.

"You look so beautiful." Mama smiled and pressed her handkerchief to the corners of her eyes. "The gown fits you perfectly."

Joy bubbled around the butterflies filling Josie's stomach. The day she'd longed for had arrived. Only one thing would make her joy complete. If only they'd make their first home in Dayton.

Her smile faltered in the mirror. How she wished Art hadn't accepted a position miles from Dayton and home. She knew the job would provide a strong start for them, an opportunity Art hadn't found in Dayton. Her dreams they'd start life in a small apartment near Mama and Daddy had evaporated. Instead, they'd head to Cincinnati. She'd longed for an adventure, and this move fit the bill. The chance to launch their life on their own was reality. While it might not have been her initial dream, a tingle of excitement edged the glow of anticipation she felt when she thought about her new life with her husband. *Husband.* She rolled the word around in her mind again and again. Heat flushed her cheeks as she thought of everything the word meant. God had blessed her!

"Josephine Miller, you'll be late to your own wedding if you don't move." Her younger sister's sharp words pulled Josie from her thoughts.

Josie cleared her throat. "Isn't that Mama's line, Kat?"

Mama laughed as Josie fiddled with the bottom of her lace jacket. It topped a floor-length, lace-covered gown that made her feel like a movie star or wealthy socialite.

Kat stood in the glow of colors flowing through the stained-glass window. They accented her athletic form and the bruise she'd acquired in her latest game with the boys. Josie shook her head. Clothing Kat in a dress didn't make the girl any less of a tomboy. Kat caught her stare and rolled her eyes. "Fine. Just remember I'm the one who told you Art was interested."

The door groaned on its hinges as it pushed into the room, making way for Carolynn Treen. Carolynn had done an amazing job pulling together the wedding of Josie's dreams. Josie's breath caught at the thought.

Carolynn shut the door behind her. "Are you ready, Josie? The organist is waiting for her cue."

"She's ready." Kat played with Josie's small bouquet before placing it back in the vase. "She can't stop fidgeting."

"I've waited a long time for this moment." Friendship followed by a courtship. Josie had known before Art asked that he was the kind of man she wanted to marry. His firm character and commitment to God made him the one she could imagine spending the rest of her life with.

"Only a few more minutes." Carolynn laughed and motioned her hand in a circle. "Twirl, Josie. Let me absorb your beauty."

Josie lowered her chin demurely as she obeyed.

"Hmmm. Art is a lucky man." Carolynn squeezed Josie and squealed. "Can you believe it? You're getting married!"

A lopsided smile stretched Kat's face. "About time. Now I get my own room."

"When you put it that way, I'm surprised you didn't push me out sooner." Josie tried to make her expression match her stern words, but couldn't. Tickles of joy pulsed through her.

It was here.

Her wedding.

The tickle turned to full-fledged, gut-splitting happiness.

She'd dreamed someday she would find a man like Art Wilson. But with the war consuming Europe, matters like love seemed trivial. She'd tried to be content helping Mama take care of the house and Daddy, Kat, and her older brother, Mark. Then she'd met Art at church. . . .

Kat snorted. "Ugh. You're thinking about him again. Let's get this wedding over. You are way too focused on him."

Oh, to be thirteen again with unlimited wisdom.

Carolynn's sweet laugh filled the room as she ruffled Kat's curls. "Someday, you'll understand. You won't be thirteen forever."

The look on Kat's face telegraphed she sincerely doubted she'd ever be as crazy about someone as Josie was for Art.

Carolynn tugged a corner of Josie's veil. "There. You look perfect. Well, I'd better get back out there and let them know you're ready."

Josie hugged Carolynn, then brushed the top of the comb holding the veil back in place. Artificial pearls dotted the top, hiding the stems of the baby's breath lining the veil.

The first notes of "Amazing Grace" filtered through the door. Mama tucked her handkerchief in her sleeve and smiled. "I'd best head in. Let them usher me to my place." She kissed Josie on the cheek and hugged her lightly, the sweet scent of violets filling the air around her. "Love you, Josephine."

Josie sucked in a deep breath and eased it out as Mama slipped from the room. She loved Art to the very core of her being. She'd been amazed to realize one could know something so important in a matter of days. He treated her like a treasured gift, someone he couldn't believe he'd wooed.

"Where's Daddy?"

"I'm here, darling." Louis Miller strode into the room, looking dapper, if professorial, in his best suit. He buttoned the final button on his double-breasted jacket that eased across his ample belly. "You look beautiful, Josephine. Art is lucky to have won you."

Peace filtered into her heart. Daddy would only give his blessing to her marriage to a man he believed would care deeply for her. "Thank you." She took a deep breath. "I can't believe I'm getting married."

"My happiest days were the day I married your mama and the days each of you kids were born. Serve and love him with all you have." Daddy's Adam's apple bobbed as he swallowed. "My prayer is that you will have a love that transforms your life like my love for your mama has me."

The music changed to the sweet strains of "It Is Well with My Soul." It might not be everybody's idea of wedding music, but every time she heard the tune, the words spoke to her soul. She longed to race through the door and up the aisle of the community church. Art and the minister would stand at the front, waiting for her.

Daddy swallowed; then he offered his arm. "It's time, Jo."

"I'm ready." She slipped her hand through his arm and closed her eyes. When she opened them, Kat slipped past her. Kat's green dress highlighted her pale complexion and the reddish highlights in her hair. Kat had taken after Mama's Irish heritage, while Josie looked more like her daddy's mother. Carolynn squeezed her hand before she moved out the door and to the sanctuary. How could she say good-bye to

Carolynn? The friend who had cried and dreamed with her?

Daddy tucked her closer to his side. Together, they stepped toward the sanctuary and her future.

❧

The music swelled from the organ, and the pastor motioned for the congregation to stand. Art Wilson marveled at the many people who filled the rows to celebrate his marriage to Josephine Miller. Many were strangers, friends of her family. His family filled one row, and a few of his college friends took another. He tugged at the sleeves of his dark suit coat. Where was his beautiful bride? The ceremony should have started by now, but every minute seemed to stretch. He'd waited a lifetime for this moment. He bounced on his toes as he tried to see over the crowd and find her.

Just one glance of her dark waves. That's all he wanted. One glimpse that solidified the fact she would soon wear his name.

Josie was marrying him. Arthur Wilson. Man with faith and hope for the future, with some money in his bank account. This new job would only improve their circumstances since it held the opportunity to provide well for her. And any kids God blessed them with. He hadn't thought his grin could get any bigger, but the thought of little Josies running around someday made his heart about explode. Yes, he was a man blessed beyond words that a woman like her could love a man like him.

There she was. He stilled, drinking in every detail. She was a vision in white lace. Her dark hair was pulled off her slender neck, and a sweet smile graced her lips, then moved to her eyes when she saw him. The light of promise filled her eyes. No woman had ever looked lovelier. Mr. Miller looked like he had a slim grip on his emotions. How hard would it be to give away a daughter? He would know someday if God gave them children. Their home would be different from the quiet one he'd grown up in. Their children would know their father's love as he bounced them on his knee. Or he'd throw one into the air just to hear the child echo Josie's delicate laugh.

"Who gives this woman to this man?" Pastor Richmond's deep voice reverberated through the sanctuary.

"I do." Mr. Miller handed Josie to him. "Take good care of her, son."

Art captured her soft hand in his. "I will, sir." He gazed into Josie's eyes. Her lips trembled at the edges as she gazed at him. "I love you, Josie."

"I love you more."

A certainty settled on him. He promised to do everything in his power to make this woman understand how much he treasured and loved her.

one

January 1940

The smell of ground beef frying in the skillet filled the kitchen. Josie grabbed a bottle of milk from the icebox and turned to the table.

"Mix the biscuits. Brown the meat." The steps to preparing the meal tripped off her tongue. Tonight they would celebrate their two-month anniversary. She wanted to make the evening special but didn't trust herself to broil steak. If only she'd paid a bit more attention when Mama had tried to teach her the finer details of cooking. Nope, she'd had to focus on housekeeping. The apartment sparkled while she slowly tried one recipe after another with varying degrees of success. She was blessed that Art played the good sport regardless of what she plopped on the table.

Warmth flooded her at the thought of Art's smile as he walked through the front door and pulled her into his embrace. She counted down to the moment he appeared. Each day, it seemed he raced home as if another moment's separation would be too much.

Two months. In her most extravagant imaginations, she hadn't pictured how wonderful marriage truly was.

She glanced around the apartment. It was small, but close enough to Art's job that he walked to the factory on all but the coldest days. While he worked, she added touches to the rooms, turning the space into a home. Grandma's davenport, decorated with a few pillows and Aunt Mary's doilies, sat against one wall in the living room. A tiny, round table—nothing like Mama's large one—filled the other corner. Josie had slipped a flowered cloth over it. The matching fabric for curtains sat on the lone chair in the bedroom. Soon, she'd buckle down and hem them. She'd made great strides in the room, but there was more she could do to make it feel like home. She turned on the radio that sat on the floor next to the couch. She'd fill the air with Glenn Miller tunes matching her celebratory mood.

As the swinging music filled the air, Josie spun around the room. She must make quite a picture. Joy bubbled inside and spilled over as she laughed.

"It's only a two-month anniversary."

If she felt this excited now, she couldn't imagine what life would be like when they hit six months. A year. Fifteen years.

ﻼ

Art glanced at his pocket watch. It felt weighty and substantial in his hand, like the expectations of the men in his family, particularly his grandfather. He'd never forget the words Grandfather spoke as he had handed the gold watch to Art at his college graduation. "You may have graduated, son, but the men in this family have each earned their way in this world, and I expect no less of you. With your education, you should do more than the others."

Do more.

No handouts.

Grandfather couldn't have been clearer. He was a self-made man and expected nothing less from Art. Forget the millions sitting in Grandfather's bank account.

A little money would have been nice as a wedding present. Help him and Josie get started. But that wasn't Grandfather's way. Art could respect that.

Art's thoughts turned back to his desk. He'd cleared about as much as he could if he still hoped to get home at a decent time. His accounting job with the E. K. Fine Piano Company was a good position. It built on the eclectic experience he'd gained at a small firm in Dayton. The difference? Now he used his education and training every day. That's what he'd wanted when he took the position.

He looked at the stack of papers and corporate books on

his desk. A weight settled in his gut. He could work for two months straight and never complete all the work. The firm had been without a bookkeeper too long. It would take forever to straighten out the mess. Yet Art also knew he should be grateful. Thanks to the weak economy, good jobs were still hard to find.

He stared at the piles of paper, but his thoughts were with his bride. Josie. Warmth filled him at the thought of her. Marriage to her exceeded his hopes. Life was richer. Not for one minute did he miss going home to a small, empty bachelor's pad each evening. He glanced at the watch again, deciding to stay a few minutes more. After all, working hard at his job *was* taking care of his bride.

"Wilson, you still here?" Edward Kendall Fine III stopped at Art's desk. The rotund man liked to emphasize the fact he was the third. Art failed to see the significance since he'd never known E. K. Fine the first or second. "Burning the midnight oil, I see. I like that in a man. Willing to work until the job's done."

Art wavered between smiling or groaning. In the few weeks he'd been at E. K. Fine's Piano Company, it had become crystal clear that E. K. Fine would squeeze everything from the men in his employ. Every last drop of work.

"Making sure I understand the complexities of the company, sir."

Mr. Fine showed his crooked teeth in what some would call a smile. "See to it you do, Wilson. This is a big company. Lots of issues to stay on top of. Keep those books clean."

Art nodded, then opened his mouth.

"Well, I'm off to see the missus. Good night."

Art closed his mouth. Surely if Mr. Fine was headed home, he could, too. The time on his watch stamped in his mind. Six o'clock. He'd have to hurry his walk or be more than an hour late. Josie would understand, wouldn't she?

❧

The dish sat on the stove, ready to pop into the oven the

moment Art walked in the door. Josie curled up on the davenport and tried to follow the flow of words as they swam across the pages of the book. Usually, Willa Cather's characters spoke to her, but tonight, every fiber seemed tuned to the door as she listened for the sound of Art's footsteps in the hallway. Her stomach grumbled its protest that it was past dinner time.

She heard the creak of one of the hall floorboards. Josie tossed the book onto the couch and stood. Brushing the wrinkles from her skirt, she hurried to the door. He was finally home! Josie pulled the apartment door open and leaned against the doorjamb. "Welcome home."

Art's hair stood up in all directions, as if he'd carelessly run his fingers through it. A smile tugged the corner of her mouth at the thought. She'd seen him make that gesture so many times.

Fatigue weighed down the corners of his eyes. "Thanks." He brushed a kiss on her cheek and pulled her into the apartment with him. "Another day in the office finished."

"Night, too." She whispered the words under her breath. Maybe he wouldn't notice.

Art stopped and looked at her. "What's that mean?"

"Nothing." Josie slid her arms around his waist. "I wish my groom were home more. It's lonely here without you."

"I miss you, too." He snuggled her closer. She giggled and pulled away.

"Let me get supper in the oven."

Art shrugged out of his coat, plopping it over the back of a chair. "Smells good."

Josie crossed her fingers. "Hope it tastes good." She drew the word out as she popped the pan in the oven. Tugging him to the couch, she sank onto its cushion. "Tell me about your day."

He leaned against the back, head tipped toward the ceiling. His words about trying to catch the company's books up-to-date flowed over her. She didn't really understand much of what he did, but that didn't matter. What did matter was that he loved what he did. And he loved her. She might be a little lonely when he was gone, but she'd do something about that eventually. Right now, she enjoyed the time to develop their relationship as it explored this new level.

"Did you get out today?"

"Just to the library and the grocer."

Art laughed. "I don't know if that qualifies since the grocer is downstairs."

"The library does. I had to walk almost a mile round trip." She shuddered in an exaggerated shiver. "It's too cold to do even that right now."

His fingers caressed her cheek. "Are you happy, Mrs. Wilson?"

"You'll have to come up with a harder question than that."

"You haven't answered me."

Josie smiled. "I can't imagine being happier."

৯

The conversation lingered in Art's mind long after dinner had been eaten and the dishes cleared. Josie seemed so content in their relationship, but he wondered about her loneliness. He didn't expect Josie to spend her days in the apartment. Yet that's what she'd done since they'd moved. He'd asked her to marry him, then transported her out of the familiar to a new world. She'd always seemed the kind who loved adventure, but maybe the reality of living in a new and different place didn't match the glamour of the idea. Her words indicated she didn't think much about it, but still, he wondered.

After work the following day, he stopped at a bookshop. She loved to read. Maybe a book would be a nice surprise gift. He ambled among the rows, trying not to sneeze through the dust that filled the air and tickled his nose. Which of the many volumes would appeal to her? She read so much he couldn't keep up with her list. It had taken her mere days to discover the library branch near their home, a find that saved them immense amounts of money. Today, though, he wanted to surprise her with a book that would be meaningful to her. Among the rows of books, he spotted a nice fat tome. *Gone with the Wind.* Maybe that would work. At least it had lots of pages. Certainly, it would fill a few of her hours.

He climbed the stairs to the apartment with a spring in his step. Running to the door, he threw it open. "Darlin', I'm home."

Silence answered. He tossed his briefcase on the floor and roamed the rooms—taking all of thirty seconds—but Josie wasn't there.

He pulled off his suit coat and then loosened his tie. Guess he'd settle in and wait. He looked at the briefcase. Maybe the thick book would work for him, too. He settled on the couch and cracked it open.

The scrape of the key in the lock pierced his mind. He rubbed his eyes and then looked at the thing weighing down his chest.

"Well, fiddle-dee-dee."

Josie swept into the room, cold-kissed roses filling her cheeks. "What was that?"

"Um, nothing." Art ran his fingers through his hair and sat up. "Where have you been?" He winced at the note of censure in his voice. "I was surprised you weren't here when I got home."

"I decided to go out. Explore the neighborhood despite the bite in the air. Eclectic architecture fills the neighborhoods around here. Brick. Wood." She pulled a beret from her head and tossed it on the table. A quirky grin—one of her best features—creased her face. "The birds beckoned me to join them." She flopped next to him on the couch.

"In the snow?" He tried to hide his skepticism, but her raised eyebrows signaled he'd failed. He put his hands up, palms out. "Okay. You've transformed into a snow princess who loves the cold. Snow White with the animals talking to you."

"As long as you think I'm the most beautiful in the land." Her face scrunched in a pout. Art couldn't resist her and didn't need to, so he reached for her and pulled her into an easy hug.

"There's no question." He tucked a loose strand of hair

behind her ear. "There's no one else for me. No one more beautiful. No one more silly." She poked him in the side. "And no one else I could love."

Josie leaned her head against his shoulder and sighed.

He pulled back. "What?"

"Nothing."

"No, my princess can't sigh like that without explaining. A prince needs the opportunity to fix his beloved's woes."

Josie giggled and shrugged. "I don't know how to explain." Oh, it hadn't taken Art long to learn those words were often the forerunner to something important. "I love the life we're building together. But some days, it feels like I'm stuck. There's got to be more to this area. If only one of the churches we've visited felt like home."

"We'll find one." Out of all the churches in Cincinnati, one had to feel like home. Someday. Until then. . . "What about ladies at the library?"

Josie crinkled her nose. "They're either old or have lots of kids. I don't exactly fit."

"Why not try?"

"Don't you miss anybody from home?"

"You're my home."

She sat up, and a winsome smile flitted across her face. "I struggle to be as content. I miss my friends. I even miss Mark and Kat. Before we moved, if you'd told me I'd miss Kat, I would have laughed. But I'd welcome her never-ending teasing right now." She wiped a tear away, and Art felt something inside tighten. "I love you, Art." He was so glad to hear those words. "I guess I didn't understand leaving would be so hard."

Art sank deeper into the couch. Someday, he'd give Josie the nice furniture she deserved. No more handouts from family. Until then, he wanted to make her happy.

"What will help you meet people? Make Cincinnati feel like home?"

"I don't know. Maybe I'll live in the library every day. Escape in a book."

Art grinned. He'd known *Gone with the Wind* was the ticket. "I got this for you today." He handed the heavy book to her. Her eyes lit up as she took it from him.

"Ah. Fiddle-dee-dee, indeed." She fanned the pages. "How much have you read?"

"Only enough to know the Tarleton twins don't stand a chance with Scarlett."

"Hmm."

"But I do with you."

She snuggled closer. "Then I think it's time to kiss me, mister."

Art couldn't think of anything he'd rather do.

two

Valentine's Day. Art would make it home on time. Something told him it would be important to Josie. Days like this he wished he'd grown up with sisters. Maybe they would have taught him the important lessons on what gals expected. Maybe then he'd better understand Josie. She was an absolute puzzle to him. One he determined he'd solve.

Tonight he'd take her to dinner. Celebrate how much he loved her and how grateful he was she'd said yes. He started to straighten the ledgers and papers overflowing on his desk until they began to resemble piles.

"Ahem." Art turned at the sound of a cleared throat.

"Yes, sir?" He stilled as he looked up at the stork-like man standing in front of his desk. He'd heard rumors that E. K. Fine II took bites out of employees with his words as he pecked away at them. The look on the man's face puzzled Art. Why would the second Mr. Fine stand in front of his desk?

"Have you followed the news in England, young man?" Mr. Fine picked up the nameplate from Art's desk. "Mr. Wilson?"

"It's hard not to."

"Yes, yes."

Art squirmed in the growing silence as Fine looked over his glasses at him. "Can I help you with something, sir?"

"We have a small plant in England, you know. I'm concerned about our workers there. Their families."

Art couldn't imagine living with the threat of Germans bombing his home in the middle of the night. Here, the renewed aerial attacks punctuated the headlines. There, the shock of air raid sirens wrenched you from sleep.

"Terrible times."

"I've never been more glad to live here."

19

Mr. Fine nodded. "Any family in England?"

"Distant cousins, I think." Art shrugged. "My mother keeps up on those family relationships."

"Well. I'll leave you to your duties." The man ambled out of the accounting department. Art watched him leave and wondered what the conversation had really been about.

He cleared the surface of his desk and smiled. The workday was over. Art punched out and walked the mile home. The best feature of their apartment was its closeness to work. Most weeks, his vehicle sat off the alley. Josie could use it if she needed, though he didn't think she ever had.

After sitting behind a desk all day, he enjoyed the feel of sunshine on his face, even as he hunkered inside his coat against the cold. He squinted at the sinking sun. Tried to imagine what it would be like to live with the fear that each time he glanced up he might see an enemy plane headed his way. And all he had to worry about was doing his job well and loving Josie. His Josie. His steps quickened at the thought of seeing her again. Their good-bye kiss this morning seemed days ago instead of mere hours.

ᘒ

Josie pushed a hand into her stomach. It hadn't stopped roiling all day. Well, there had been moments she'd felt normal. Then she'd smell something, and her stomach betrayed her again. She couldn't think of anything she'd eaten that would make her feel this way. She should get supper started but grimaced at the thought and covered her mouth to still the nausea.

Maybe a salad would work. No scents involved there. She opened the icebox door and stared inside. Nothing appealed to her.

The apartment door groaned as it swung open.

"I'm home." Art's boisterous voice filled the small rooms.

Josie took a deep breath and steeled herself before turning around. Maybe if she was stern enough with it, her stomach would cooperate. "Hi, honey. Good day?"

"A fine one. But the best part is we're going out for dinner.

The cook gets the night off as we celebrate Valentine's Day with a steak, maybe see a movie, then a kiss." He waggled his eyebrows and smiled, the one that normally sent a flood of warmth through her. Instead, Josie clutched her stomach and tried not to groan at the thought of food. His face fell. "Don't want to go out on the town? I thought you'd enjoy that. We can even see that cartoon *Pinocchio* if you want."

The pout in his voice made her smile. "I would love it."

The smile reappeared on his face.

Josie sighed. "But I haven't felt very well all day."

"Do we need to get you to the doctor?"

Josie laughed. "That's not necessary. Just a touchy stomach. I bet I'm better by tomorrow. Do you mind if we stay in tonight? I'll heat some soup, and then we can spend a quiet evening together."

"As long as you don't pull out one of your puzzles."

"All right. I'll let you read *Gone with the Wind* to me, instead."

"Fiddle-dee-dee." He pushed his hand against his heart and grinned. "Anything to make my lady feel better." He pulled her toward him. "Just don't tell anybody about this."

"And who would I tell?" She snuggled next to him, close enough to hear the steady beat of his heart. "It's our secret." Josie wasn't sure it would make her feel better, but it might distract her. If nothing else, watching all-male Art reading a romance would take her mind off her crazy stomach. And maybe tomorrow they could go out.

Art leaned down until his forehead touched hers. He gazed into her eyes as if searching for her very heart. Didn't he know he'd claimed it the moment he swept into the Dayton theater with his grandma on his arm? It had been Christmas time, a showing of the *Nutcracker*. Josie hadn't taken her eyes off him as she watched him guide his grandma through the crowd. He'd been so chivalrous toward the woman. It didn't hurt that his hair was the color of a dark chocolate bar and curled ever so slightly around his ears. Josie must have caught his eye, too, since he'd made his way to her side. That had been the first of their many interactions. Through them all, she'd learned while he was easy to look at, his heart was even better.

An easy smile reached his eyes.

She tried to catch her breath at his intensity. "Find what you're looking for?"

"Um-hm." He leaned in and captured her lips with his.

ᴥ

The next morning, Josie struggled to get out of bed. The warmth of the comforter seemed to push her down. The pillow snuggled against her cheek, making it hard to lift her head. She'd wanted to see Art off to his job with a smile and a kiss, but couldn't find the energy. Her stomach roiled at the thought of doing anything, and fatigue overwhelmed her. Ugh. She had to do something. Sitting in bed wasn't a valid option. Her mother's voice echoed in her mind, telling her idle hands are the devil's tools. Josie had never liked the phrase, but since the move, she hadn't worked hard to stay busy.

Maybe a job would help. Give her a schedule beyond getting dinner on the table for Art. An important task, but not enough to keep her mind engaged all day. Only a few days a week, though. She curled up in the bed and tugged Grandma's quilt to her chin. Her fingers played with the edge of the soft fabric. Some of her earliest memories involved sitting on the floor, playing while Grandma and her friends stitched quilt after quilt. Josie had hoped one day she would receive one. Now she had the one that had graced Grandma and Grandpa's bed for years. The wedding ring pattern testified to the hours of love Grandma had poured into its making. Each stitch was filled with the hope and commitment of the decades Grandma and Grandpa loved. Now, Josie and Art could add to that legacy.

Such a rich heritage.

Josie's hand pressed into her stomach. She rubbed it in small circles, trying to ease the waves of nausea.

Her mind wandered through the reasons she could feel so poorly. It didn't seem like the flu. She hadn't had any fevers— just the uncomfortable sensation. A shivery feeling collided with the butterflies. A pulse of hope and fear. It couldn't be what she thought, could it?

Well, only one way to know for sure. Taking a deep breath, she called the doctor and made an appointment. She considered walking the couple miles to the office, then opted for the trolley. After she climbed on, she decided the Packard would have been a better choice. The swaying and clacking of the trolley kept her stomach bobbing and weaving.

After a few stops, the trolley reached the intersection nearest the office. Josie hopped down and entered the office. Once checked in, she flipped through a stack of *Saturday Evening Post*s as she waited. Nothing distracted her from the only possibility that made sense.

What would she do if the doctor told her she could expect a baby to join her family? She took a deep breath and willed her heart rate to slow. She and Art wanted children. It would be wonderful news to hear that their family would start now. She'd push past the fear of what had happened to Aunt Gertie. If she'd been at a hospital, she and the baby would have survived, and that was years ago. Now things were different. And Cincinnati hospitals were much better equipped if an emergency arose.

"Mrs. Wilson?" The nurse stood at the door. Josie gathered her purse and coat. "This way please."

Josie followed her, unsure why she felt so certain of the answer. Her mother would think she was crazy to come see the doctor over something as simple and routine as a baby. But she needed to know. Was she crazy? Or was her body trying to tell her something?

The doctor bustled into the area. "How can I help you?"

"I think I'm pregnant."

"Congratulations. That's great news." He studied her. "Isn't it?"

"Yes." She took a steadying breath and matched his smile.

"How can I know for sure?"

After the examination, Josie pulled her clothes on and collected her thoughts. Waves of excitement pushed aside her earlier fears. It wouldn't be her and Art alone for long.

She returned home, trying to figure out how to share the news with Art. He'd been so eager to start a family, talking constantly about having children from the day he'd asked her to marry him. This moment should be one he remembered, but nothing came to her. It felt like her mind had turned into a blank canvas. She stood at the sink, trying to prepare something for dinner. The water dripped in the dishpan, but Josie didn't notice until drops landed on her foot. She turned off the faucet, grabbed a dishtowel, and wiped up the puddle. The front door banged against the wall, and Josie jumped, cracking her head against the sink. "Ouch."

"Is the loveliest bride in the world home?" Art's voice teased as he strode into the kitchen.

Josie rubbed her head and tried to clear the fog.

Art leaned in for a kiss. He stopped before he claimed her lips. "How was your day?"

"Wonderful." A purr slipped into her voice, and she watched his face contort in hopeful confusion. Hmm, maybe she needed to work on how she welcomed him. "But probably not as exciting as yours." If only he knew. . .

"Another day marshalling pages of numbers into order. Love the routine of getting them to line up and flow across the pages." He rubbed his hands together and then stepped back to lean against the table. He sniffed the air. "Want to go out to celebrate tonight since nothing's started?"

A burning sensation squeezed her throat. No. She swallowed and smiled. Tonight they would celebrate the beginning of their dreams. And somehow she'd manage to keep the food down. In time, this too would pass, replaced by the other sensations of a baby. Inside her.

His thumb brushed her cheek. She leaned into his hand. "I'd love to celebrate. Give me a few minutes, okay?"

He nodded and pulled his hand away. She felt a chill and hurried to the bedroom. Josie eased to the vanity and brushed her hair, then touched up her makeup. A fresh light shone from her eyes. She couldn't wait to hear Art's reaction. Something in his only child upbringing made him hungry for the patter of little feet. She couldn't imagine a better gift to give him. After they pulled on coats, he escorted her down the stairs and to the Packard. "Where would my lovely lady like to eat?"

Josie shook her head. "Oh no. You get to surprise me."

She leaned back and closed her eyes as the Packard rolled over the streets. Art stroked her hand with his thumb. She almost purred all over again. The car slowed, and she opened her eyes. Warm lights spilled from a storefront, surrounded by others shrouded in darkness. The light played off the snow drifts along the sidewalk. Art helped her from the car and led her to the door. A woman met them as they entered.

"Right this way."

Josie settled into a chair that Art pushed in for her. The small dining room was filled with bistro tables and patrons. A spicy aroma wafted from the kitchen. A waitress walked by with several plates of food, and Josie's stomach flipped as the scent got stronger. She swallowed and pressed a hand against her stomach, urging it to cooperate.

Art looked at her, a question in his gaze. "Are you okay?"

Josie nodded but kept her lips sealed, afraid to speak.

"Maybe you need to see a doctor?"

"I did." Heat eased up her cheeks at the thought.

"What?"

"I saw a doctor this afternoon." Josie took a breath. How to make this moment everything he wanted?

Art worried his lower lip between his teeth. "You'd better tell me, Josie. Nothing can be as bad as all this."

"No, this is wonderful news. Art, know how you always talk about wanting to be a dad?" A glimpse of hope flashed on his face. Josie didn't want to hide her smile any longer.

"I'm pregnant." Art's mouth dropped, and a big grin cracked his face.

"Really?"

Josie nodded as tears slipped down her cheeks. Her dream of becoming a mother, having children to dote on, was coming true.

He reached toward her as if to pull her into his arms but couldn't reach her around the table. "That's wonderful news, Josie."

Josie swiped at her cheeks. "I know. I thought we could have some time to be us, but God had different plans. I'll be more excited when I don't feel sick." He shared her excitement, and Josie loved Art all over again. This baby came straight from God's hand. The thought stilled her racing heart. God had decided this was the time for her to be a mommy. Excitement escalated inside her. "I've always loved babies."

Art scooted his chair around the table and pulled her into his arms, resting his chin on her head. "Wow. It'll be great. And you'll feel better soon, right?"

"Yes, Dr. Nathan said likely in a few weeks." That was definitely good news. She couldn't wait for her stomach to settle. The sooner the better. Yesterday would have been great. A smile spread on her face. Soon she'd walk the baby in a carriage. And the cradle could fit in the corner of the bedroom.

"We'll be great parents to the little guy."

If the giddy look on Art's face served as any indication, then she had nothing to fear. The bubble of excitement expanded. They were really going to be parents. She couldn't stop her grin. "What's that about a little boy? It might be a girl."

Art leaned back and looked into her eyes. "Either will be fine, as long as the little girl looks like her mommy."

"I'm going to be a mommy." Her voice shook on the words.

"You'll be wonderful." A feather soft kiss touched her brow.

three

The wind carried the whisper of spring as Josie walked to the library a month later. That morning, she'd woken up and not felt the need to rush to the bathroom. She reveled in the lack of nausea. What a miracle to watch the world wake up with new life around her as a child grew inside her.

Her steps bounced as she walked into the small library. The air was cool and musty. She pulled her coat close and wrinkled her nose against the dust. Why did that combination always make her thoughts turn to learning? Exploring the great books. Traveling to new destinations. Seeing life through fresh eyes. She surveyed the stacks, wondering where to start.

"Good morning, Josephine." Miss Adelaide sat behind the checkout counter, back ramrod straight, face set in proper lines. "How are you this morning?"

"Wonderful."

Miss Adelaide frowned at the loud sound. "Shh, dear." Her eyes scanned the tiny lobby area. "We aren't the only ones here."

"Sorry, Miss Adelaide." Josie tried to rein in her enthusiasm to the appropriate subdued level. "It's a beautiful day outside. Hints of spring fill the air."

"Delightful. Now what can I help you with today?" Miss Adelaide pushed out of the chair and took a step toward the fiction section. "Interested in another Jane Austen novel?"

"No." Heat crept into her cheeks. "I'd like one on baby development."

"Josephine Wilson. Are you in the family way?"

"Yes, ma'am." Josie couldn't keep the smile from exploding on her face. Didn't want to. Butterflies of excitement tickled her inside, welcome relief from the unsettling sensations.

"That is good news. Good news indeed." Miss Adelaide hurried as fast as her shuffle allowed toward the opposite side of the room from the one Josie usually perused. "Over against this wall, we have a small section of child development books. Personally, I'm not sure there's much wisdom in them. You'll find all you need in the Good Book."

"Yes, ma'am. I still wouldn't mind checking out a few books, though. There's so much I don't know."

Miss Adelaide ran her arthritic fingers along the spines of a row of books. "Didn't you tell me once that you've got siblings?" Josie nodded, though Miss Adelaide didn't wait for her response. "Then you know everything you need. Babies are simple. Love them, feed them, and keep them clean."

Josie wondered. Could it really be that simple? But Miss Adelaide grew up in a simpler time. Before life became modern. Complex. "How many children do you have?"

"Oh, I wasn't granted the blessing of having any. I helped my sisters with their broods. Auntie Adelaide to the rescue. Seventeen times."

"Oh my."

"There were a bunch of nieces and nephews, but I love them as if they were my own." She pulled out a book and handed it to Josie. "Well, here you go. If you need anything, you know where to find me. Congratulations again, dear."

"Thank you." Josie watched Miss Adelaide for a moment then turned to the book in her hand. She really wanted a book that could give her a window to what was happening inside her. Did anyone really know? Or was it a mystery reserved for God alone to know? After spending half an hour flipping through the few books the library's collection held, Josie decided the mystery must be God's.

Maybe she'd grab *Sense and Sensibility* after all.

❧

Art couldn't wait to race home and grab Josie in a huge hug. The bigger the hug, the more likely the little Wilson could sense it, right? He would have never guessed he'd become such a sap about a baby. No question about it. He loved the idea of a little one to throw in the air. Josie told him it would be awhile before the baby was big enough. But the images of all the things the two of them would do together already played through his mind. Teaching the baby to fish, solving math problems, and showing the child the wonders of God's world. Maybe even leading the child into his own relationship with the Savior. Art resisted the moisture that tinged his eyes at the thought. A strong children's Sunday school program joined the priority list for their new church home.

Was there any greater trust than having a child?

He couldn't imagine one.

And to think three months ago the idea of adding children to their family had seemed like a distant mirage. Now the anticipation stayed with him throughout the day. It seemed the most natural thing for their growing family.

"Another good day, Art."

He looked up to see Stan Jacobs standing next to his desk. Stan filled the space like an ex-college lineman.

"Yep. Now to race home."

"You should join us for a drink before heading home. Time to join the guys. Hasn't the honeymoon worn off?" A slight leer tipped Stan's mouth.

"Not for me." Art couldn't imagine losing the excitement of racing home to see his Josie after a long day apart. He wanted to hear all about her day. And be back in her arms. Yep, that's where he belonged. Not at Rosie's Bar.

"So you say now. Wait till you have your first real fight. Right, boys?"

Art hadn't noticed the other guys from the office gather round. A couple shook their heads at Stan while they grabbed their briefcases. "We don't have that kind of marriage, Stan."

The man snickered, and Art balled his fists. Where did Stan get the idea he could tell Art about marriage? It wasn't like Art had asked for advice.

"Ignore Stan." Charlie Sloan socked Stan in the shoulder. "This big lug doesn't know the wonders of married life. My wife and I've been married twenty-three years. I'd still rather be with her after a long day at work than anything else. And you're right. Drink never solved any problems."

Stan shook his head and stepped away from Art's desk. "Have it your way. But don't be surprised when I say, 'Told ya so.' She'll weigh you down." He winked at Art, then headed toward the door. "Anyone else ready for Rosie's? Come on." Several of the guys joined him as he left.

Charlie shook his head. "That boy's gonna fall mighty hard one of these days. When he does, the earth's gonna shake."

Art wanted to ask what was going to make him fall: drinking or a woman? It didn't really matter, though. "Any advice for this guy?"

"On married life?"

"Yep."

"Make sure you keep your walk with God first." Art cringed at the reminder. They needed to settle on a church home. "Most of our challenges I created when I forgot to put God first. Amazing how quickly my perspective turned sour." Charlie put a hand on Art's shoulder. "Better get home to the missus now. It's been a long day away from her."

Art grabbed his briefcase, jacket, and hat from his desk. "Sounds good to me."

The week passed in a blur of routine. Life the way he liked it. Work hard while he was at the factory office. Then spend his evenings at home with Josie. Now that she felt good again, they'd walk the neighborhood after dinner when the weather cooperated. He couldn't wait to push the baby's carriage around the block. He could already see the neighbors oohing and aahing over the little boy. Josie kept teasing him that the baby could be a girl, but he knew.

Friday night, he hurried home ready for a quiet weekend. The moment he stepped through the door, he sensed something wasn't right. Josie lay curled in a ball on the small couch.

Her arms wrapped around her middle, a tight look on her face. She moaned, eyes squeezed shut. He dropped his briefcase by the door and rushed toward her.

"Josie, honey, what's wrong?" He studied her face, his concern building when he saw tears on her cheeks. He brushed one away, trying to read her face. Why wasn't she saying anything? Pressure built inside him. Something was wrong. Looking at her face, terribly wrong. "Josie?"

She opened her mouth. Screwed it shut. Looked at him, and a sob welled from somewhere deep inside her.

"Baby, it's okay. Whatever's wrong, we'll fix." Somehow he would. He promised himself he would. No matter how much it cost. He'd fix it, since the sight of her like this tore him apart.

&

Josie tried to stop her tears, but they flowed. She'd never known fear like this. The cramps had started around noon. She hadn't thought much about them, but they grew in intensity. Right before Art got home, she'd felt the rush of blood. She wanted to protect the baby but had no idea what to do. All she could do was curl into a ball and wait for the next contraction. The helplessness crushed her.

Shouldn't she do something? Mothers protected their children.

She groaned as another cramp squeezed her middle. This was not supposed to happen.

"Josie?" Art's voice quivered, far from his usual strong tone. "Talk to me. Please."

God, where are You?

She needed His peace. Right now. Before she pulled too far inside herself trying to protect something beyond her power and ability.

"Baby?"

Her heart broke at that word. Sobs replaced the stream of tears. Art grabbed her, pulled her tight to his chest. "I'm taking you to the hospital. Now."

She tucked her face against his chest. Tried to pretend everything would be okay. But as she felt another gush of blood, she knew it would never be okay again.

ॐ

Dr. Nathan walked into her hospital room. Sorrow replaced his usual grin. "I'm sorry, Josie. There was nothing we could do."

Tears trickled down her cheeks again, as a sense of disbelief vied with certainty. Her baby was gone.

"You should be able to have other children."

The words, intended to comfort, only intensified the pain. The last thing she wanted to think about was other children. Right now, all she wanted was her baby. The one she would never hold. A sob slipped out. She sealed her lips tight against the threat of more.

Art moved his chair closer to the bed, grabbed her hand, and held tight. "I called your mom and dad. She'll see about coming but didn't sound optimistic. Something about your grandma."

Josie nodded. She didn't really expect her parents to come. What could they do? The pregnancy probably hadn't seemed real to them, after all. It had only solidified for her with the doctor visit and recent baby flutters. Art stroked her hair, but she couldn't look at him.

"We'll keep you overnight, and then you can go home." Dr. Nathan looked at her chart, then turned to leave. "I'm sorry. There's nothing we can do in situations like this."

As soon as the doctor left, Art slipped onto the bed beside her. He held her, and she felt tears fall on her. "I'm so sorry, Josie." His words were broken. His dreams, too, had died. What had she done to cause this pain for him? He'd never been anything but excited about having a baby. She wanted to yell at the heavens. Didn't God know? She'd wanted this baby. Now that the baby was gone, desperation filled her. Didn't He understand?

four

Even though Josie insisted she could walk, Art swept her up and carried her from the backseat of the Packard into the apartment. After he ignored her protests, she'd gone still, almost listless. They'd lost a child, but now he felt like he was losing her, too. She'd retreated so far inside herself he wasn't sure how to find her.

How could it hurt so much to lose one they'd never met? And with Josie lost in a place she'd created, he didn't have anyone to share the pain with. What should he do? This was virgin territory for him. So he prayed. Surely God knew exactly what they each needed to move forward. There would be other children. Art had no doubt of that. But that didn't erase his pain.

No, if anything, the pain led him straight back to the main question. *Why?* God could have prevented the loss. But He hadn't.

"Here we are, Josie. Do you want to lie down in the bedroom?"

She didn't respond. She burrowed deeper into his chest. He eased on to the couch and settled her next to him. Dr. Nathan had said she'd be back to normal in a few days. Maybe physically, but Art wondered about the rest of her.

In this unchartered water, he desperately wished someone could hand him a map.

◦

Josie tried to rouse herself. Art needed her to pull out of the pain. Could she share the depth of where her thoughts took her? Had they lost the baby because of something she'd done? Had she not been excited enough? Not appreciated the growing gift inside her?

Her thoughts were at war. Her head told her it was non-sense. But her heart felt bruised. Josie needed a reason, but there was none.

Dr. Nathan had said it was too early to know whether the baby was a girl or a boy. She'd had dreams of a little girl dressed in pleated dresses with hair a mess of blond curls. Art had sounded so certain it was a miniature him. It hadn't really mattered, though, because in a few months they'd know. Now she wondered. Was it a daughter or a son she'd never hold? She felt tears fight for release, but she refused to succumb. She'd done nothing but cry since the cramps had begun. She gritted her teeth until her jaw ached, but tears trickled down her cheeks anyway. Yet another sign of her body betraying her.

Art rubbed small circles in her shoulders and upper back. She relaxed against him. She had done nothing to deserve his gentleness, yet he continued to pour out his love on her. So like Jesus serving others.

"Read me something." The words squeaked out. A plea for something to soothe her.

The kneading slowed. "What would you like?"

"Anything full of hope." How she needed that.

He reached for the Bible on the small side table. She turned her head to watch him flip through the gently worn pages. "How about a Psalm?" Without waiting for her acquiescence, he began reading.

" 'Be merciful unto me, O God: for man would swallow me up; he fighting daily oppresseth me.' " Art's rich baritone reached deep inside her, making her believe because he believed. " 'What time I am afraid, I will trust in thee. In God I will praise his word, in God I have put my trust; I will not fear what flesh can do unto me.' " Oh, how she needed that: the certainty that she could trust in the God she'd praised all her life. Surely, He was still there, still worthy of praise even when her heart was broken.

" 'Thou tellest my wanderings: put thou my tears into thy bottle: are they not in thy book? When I cry unto thee, then shall mine enemies turn back: this I know; for God is for me.'"

God *was* for her. What a comforting thought. She could trust that promise. She *would* trust that promise. Despite what her heart felt at that moment in time. God was for her.

" 'In God will I praise his word: in the Lord will I praise his word. In God have I put my trust: I will not be afraid what man can do unto me. Thy vows are upon me, O God: I will render praises unto thee. For thou hast delivered my soul from death: wilt not thou deliver my feet from falling, that I may walk before God in the light of the living?'"

Fresh tears wet her cheeks as she listened to the familiar words of Psalm 56. God held all of her tears. The thought was somehow comforting. He had never promised that her life would be pain free. As she wiped her cheeks, how she wished He had. No, He'd promised He would value each tear she cried. What an amazing—and absolutely humbling—thought. The God of the universe cared enough to watch and collect each tear.

A strange, unexpected peace washed over her. She might not see how, but she knew with a certainty they would make it to the other side of this valley. As Art's voice continued to roll over her in soothing waves, Josie relaxed against the couch and him.

&

A soft kiss on her cheek pulled Josie from darkness. Confusion swirled through her mind. Where was she? Art must have moved her into their room at some point during the night.

"I've got to get to work, baby." Art leaned over her, dressed, with his tie jumbled around his neck and a hat slapped on his head. "Will you be okay?"

Josie nodded. What else could she do? He had to work. And she'd find a way out of the morass pulling her back to the blackness. Trails of peace that had teased her had evaporated during the night. Art's rough fingers stroked her cheek before he kissed her again.

"I'll hurry home. I love you." He waited a moment, then stood.

She licked her lips, as she tried to find her voice. "Love you."

The door closed behind him, and she turned back into her pillow. She prayed sleep would come. She wasn't ready to face the day and her emptiness.

⁂

"Hello." A soft voice trilled into the apartment.

Josie looked up from the book she held in her lap. She'd read no more than four pages in the hours since she had crawled out of bed, her thoughts lost in the land of what-ifs.

"I hope it's all right I came in." A familiar older woman stepped into the living room, a smile softening her wrinkled face and a basket hanging from her arm. "That fine young man of yours asked if I'd look in on you. I don't know if you remember my name—I'm Doris Duncan. My husband, Scott, owns the market, and we live below you on the second floor."

The woman had always been friendly, but in the several months they'd lived here, she hadn't ventured up the last flight of stairs to this apartment. Josie stiffened her defenses. She didn't want to spend time with a stranger. "That isn't necessary. I'm fine."

"I'm sure you are. But I brought a light lunch anyway. I love an excuse to get out of my place."

Josie bit back a bitter protest, but the deep growl of her stomach silenced her. Betrayer. The last thing she wanted to think about was food. Yet as Doris pulled items from the basket, a sweet honeyed aroma wafted toward her. Maybe she could eat something. She struggled off the couch and moved the few steps to the kitchen. "Here are some plates."

"Perfect. Here, settle down." Mrs. Duncan placed several small bowls on the round dining table. Finally, she unearthed a cloth-wrapped bundle that could only be sweet rolls, the source of the wonderful scent. "My mama's special recipe. They always comfort me whenever I need an extra reminder of love." Her easy movements stilled as she eyed Josie. "Here. Sit, child. You look weak around the edges."

Josie sank onto a chair and waited. Doris had something to say, otherwise why come? They weren't exactly friends, barely acquaintances, hardly even neighbors. Watching Doris made her want her mama. The hollow in her heart longed for Mama to hold her and tell her everything would be okay. But Mama hadn't made the drive, and the ache remained.

"Where would I find the silverware?"

"The drawer next to the sink."

Doris flitted back to the table and then settled on a chair. She reached across the small table for Josie's hand. "Let's pray first." Without waiting for Josie's response, she bowed her head. "Father, we come before You. You are a holy and awesome God. But You are also the God who experiences our pain with us. As my neighbor walks through this time, I ask that You surround her with Your love and shelter her in Your arms. Give her hope, Lord. And help her believe You have nothing but good plans for her."

Josie stiffened at the thought. If He really had only good plans for her, why this loss? It certainly didn't meet her definition of good.

Stillness settled in the room, and Doris did not release her hand. Peace relaxed Doris's face, and she tilted her head to the side as if hearing something special. Josie waited, fatigue settling over her like a heavy blanket. Oh, for some peace. Instead, she wanted to curl up in a ball and pretend the last twenty-four hours hadn't happened. Yep, hiding would solve all her problems. And who was she to think she had problems when bombs fell in Europe? People died, while others lost their homes and livelihoods. She sat in a small, comfortable apartment, with a husband who had a good job. All their needs were cared for, and they even had enough for wants. She should feel blessed. Instead, her arms felt empty. Empty of the child she hadn't understood how much she wanted until the baby was gone.

"You'll pull through this, Mrs. Wilson. You're made of strong stock. You may not ever forget, but you will not live in this place with this loss unless you choose." Doris's voice filled with strength and a knowing.

Josie studied her, then looked at her plate. Even the sweet roll tasted like sawdust. "You've experienced this. . .loss." The word stuck in her throat. It was so inadequate. "Haven't you?"

Doris's faded blue eyes glistened with what looked like tears. She looked out the window, fixing her gaze on nothing Josie could see. "It was thirty-two years ago. We'd been married a year. Both so thrilled to have a baby on the way. Well, the baby embraced Jesus before we held him." A single tear trailed down her weathered cheek. "I won't say I don't still feel the knowing I've missed a lifetime with that child. But eternity is so much longer." She looked at Josie, peace reflecting in the tears. "I will see him on the other side. And we'll have so much to catch up on."

"I don't want to wait." Josie tried to hide her broken heart in the angry words.

"I know. But as with many areas in life, we may never understand the why now. Until then, I trust God." Sadness tinged Doris's face. "It's been thirty-two years, and many of my questions remain unanswered. But I know I will see that child one day. And then this time will seem insignificant in light of eternity."

❧

Art hurried home from work. The day had dragged as his thoughts returned home with worries about Josie. Should he have made an excuse to stay home? He had to work, provide for her, especially at a time when life seemed unfair. Had he done the right thing asking Mrs. Duncan to check on her? He thought so but wondered how Josie had reacted. She could be feisty when backed into a corner. He prayed she hadn't felt that way.

When he reached home, Josie sat on the couch in her nightgown, her hair pulled out of her face, her features drawn.

She held a handkerchief against her cheek as she watched him walk in.

"Hey." He sank onto the couch next to her.

She leaned away from him, but he edged closer. She couldn't force him away, not when she needed him. She might not understand it yet, but they would walk through this together. They'd both lost a child.

But they would not lose each other.

five

Warmth brushed Josie's face. She cracked open her eyelids, struggling against the weight pushing her farther into the bed. In the days and weeks since the loss, the bed had called her name, urging her to spend daylight hours ensconced there. The fight seemed futile. Rays of April sunshine teased her through a crack in the curtains. If she opened the windows, the scent of hyacinths would filter into the room. Instead, she burrowed deeper under the comforter, practically pulling it over her head.

She reached out for Art, but he was gone. Long enough that his side of the bed felt cold. The aroma of coffee filtered through the door. The scent tweaked her heart. She should have gotten up before Art left for work, should have made his breakfast like she used to. She closed her eyes against the fresh well of pain. His life continued—the normal cycle of work and home.

Yet she felt trapped. Stripped of her dreams. Filled with what-ifs. What-might-have-beens. They echoed through her mind. She knew God had more for her than this, but relief from the thoughts only came as she slipped into sleep.

Minutes passed as she tried to force herself back to sleep.

"Enough." The muffled word didn't carry much force, but it propelled her out of bed. Slipping her robe on, she stumbled out of the bedroom, through the small living room, into the kitchen. Josie reached to tie the robe shut, then stopped as her hands brushed her stomach. Pain cramped through her, and she tried to catch her breath against it. What should be softly rounded remained all too flat. Her hands trembled as she dumped the coffee, then filled the pot with water and set it on the stove. She waited for waves of anger to overtake the pain as it had many mornings. Instead, the ache spread until she could almost feel the weight of the baby she would never hold. Lips compressed tight against the sob wanting to escape, she grabbed her Bible from the counter where it had collected dust since the frantic dash to the hospital. She fluctuated between resignation and anger-laced questions directed at the heavens.

She stroked the worn cover and sank to the couch, wondering if she dared open it. Josie almost didn't want to know what God wanted to say to her. The words brought such comfort when Art read them, yet marched across the page like angry ants whenever she tried to read.

Maybe she didn't want to hear anything.

Especially from a God who hadn't held her when she needed Him most.

Her thoughts spiraled back to the pain.

He could have prevented the miscarriage.

She should feel the flutters of life deep inside her.

The feeling of betrayal wouldn't leave. He was God. He could have stopped it. He should have stopped it. And if He had—she pressed a hand against her stomach desperate to stop the anger that filled her—things would be so different.

Her pulse raced. He'd disappeared when she needed Him. She'd lain on the couch and begged Him to be with her, but instead, she'd spun like a child who'd lost her father in the chaos of a state fair carnival. No matter how she searched for Him, she couldn't find Him.

Breathing in shallow gasps, she knew the fear couldn't be more real. She'd never felt so abandoned.

"Knock, knock." The words trilled through the opening door. Josie tried to scrub the pain from her face as Doris slipped into the room. The soft scent of cinnamon filled the room just as Doris had filled a void in her life. She'd become a constant through the fog of Josie's questions and life-stopping pain. Even when she pushed Josie to focus on Art and what she had, Doris had become a welcome part of Josie's life. Her persistence had edged their relationship from strangers to acquaintances to friends.

Josie had ached for a friend. And then Doris appeared. Art should probably thank Doris for keeping her from completely losing her way.

"How are you doing this morning?" Doris smiled at Josie as if it was the most natural thing in the world to find her in a nightgown and robe with unbrushed hair at ten o'clock in the morning. "I brought over some of my cinnamon bread. Fresh baked this morning. Did the smell tempt you from bed? Nothing smells better to me in the morning. Well, that lilac tree outside our windows might."

Just when Josie wondered if Doris would ever slow down and wait for a response, she stopped and smiled. "Listen to me chatter. I must like the sound of my own voice this morning." She nodded to the book Josie held. "Glad to see you looking at that. The answers you seek rest between its covers."

"You're right." It was easier to admit it than argue with the woman. It wasn't Doris's fault that God has gone conspicuously silent. "Maybe someday I'll find them." Josie slapped her hand over her mouth. "I didn't mean to say that."

Laugh lines crinkled the corners of Doris's eyes. "Of course you did. And that sentiment doesn't surprise God at all. Go ahead and tell Him exactly what you think and feel. I doubt you'll surprise Him."

The lady had a point. "All right." The teakettle whistled, and Josie stood. "Would you like some?"

"Yes. I'll get plates for our bread." As soon as they were settled back at the table, Doris grabbed Josie's hands and bowed her head. After a quick prayer, she looked at Josie and smiled. "As soon as we're done here, get dressed. You and I are going out."

Josie frowned. The last thing she wanted was to leave. Doris tipped her chin and stared her down.

"You're not getting out of this, young lady, so you might as well give in graciously. It's time to get your thoughts off yourself." A smile softened the words' edges. Doris winked at her, then took a bite. A few minutes later, the bread had disappeared along with the tea. "Scoot. I'll clean up the kitchen while you get ready."

Seemed she had no options. Josie stood and headed to her room. She slipped into a gingham dress and pulled her hair into a simple twist. Even those little actions made her feel better, more in control. She slapped a hat on her head and grabbed a purse. Squaring her shoulders, she rejoined Doris.

"Much better." Doris tugged her toward the door. "You'll be glad you came."

"Yes, ma'am." What else could she say? Doris had made up her mind.

They stepped onto the sidewalk, and the sun felt wonderful. It warmed Josie, and a bubble of something sweet filled her.

"Don't analyze that too closely, dear. You'll be surprised by hope on even your darkest days. God has a way of doing that." Doris kept the pace brisk as they walked several blocks. Josie hurried her steps to keep up, watching for signs of spring. The scent of the season of new life, a heady mix of hyacinth and tulips, filled her senses.

"Ah. Here we are." Doris led her into a church. Josie tried to find the name, but Doris pulled her in, much faster than she'd expected the older woman to move. The urgency in her steps pulled at Josie's curiosity. What had her so excited? "This is one of my favorite days of the week. There's something wonderful about God using me to serve others." As she talked, she led Josie along a hallway and then down some stairs. The aroma of something spicy tickled Josie's nose and collided with the smell of unwashed bodies as they walked into a large, open room. Josie struggled not to grimace at the mix of odors and what it did to her breakfast.

"What are we doing?"

"Caring for others. Today's the day my church serves the needy through the soup kitchen. Someday, we may open every day, but until then, we share the need with other churches." As she walked, Doris brushed the arm of a man seated at one of the tables. "How are you today, Bruce?"

"I'm still alive, ma'am."

"That's good, real good. Make sure you get your soup and bread."

"Yes, ma'am."

The next hours flew as Doris put Josie to work pouring vegetable soup into bowls too numerous to count. She tried to ignore the fact that many of the women coming through were large with child. She tried to smile even as a knife cut into her heart. Gritting her teeth, she kept the tears from falling. And as she focused on those in front of her with immediate needs, a dream slowly reawakened in her heart, one she'd shoved into a hidden corner. Images of the times she'd helped her mother in settings like this. When the whole family had pulled together the extras they had to share with the less fortunate. And there had been so many during the hard days of the '30s. While she'd thought those times had passed, today reopened her eyes to the need. Maybe she could play a part in meeting those needs, serving as Jesus instructed His followers. And maybe as she took her eyes off her hurt, she'd move beyond the grief.

❧

Art hurried home. Today, the numbers had swum in front of his eyes, not sliding into ordered columns like usual. He tried to take in the song of the birds as they flew about, looking for nest materials. Instead, his thoughts fixated on Josie. It had been weeks since they lost the baby, yet it seemed as fresh to her as yesterday. If he came home to find her still in her nightgown again, he didn't know what he'd do.

Shouldn't he be enough?

He shook his head. He clearly wasn't enough for Josie. The thought pained him. They'd only been married a few months, and already she needed more. He cringed and tried to rein in his thoughts. He knew Jesus was the only One who should be her all in all, but it would have been nice to think he mattered, too.

Art's steps slowed as he approached the grocery store. Mr. Duncan pushed a broom back and forth across the sidewalk. "Afternoon."

"Sir."

"How's the missus?" Scott's eyes softened at the edges.

"She's. . . I don't know. I thought she'd be back to normal." The word didn't quite fit, but he didn't know how else to explain the situation. "Is she home?"

"Doris took her out on a service project, but they've been back for a while." Scott leaned on his broom handle. "Can I offer a piece of advice, advice learned the hard way?"

Art nodded.

"Be gentle with her. This pain you've both had. . .well, it's different for a woman. Seems more personal in ways we can't understand."

"Yes, sir."

"Keep loving her. It's the best thing you can do."

Art nodded and climbed the stairs to the apartment. He almost rapped on his door, just to make sure she knew he'd arrived. "Hey, honey."

Josie looked up from her book and smiled at him. He looked closer. Sadness still edged her eyes, but the smile seemed more real.

"Welcome home." She tilted her head for his kiss, then patted the couch next to her. "How was your day?"

"A little off actually." A frown creased her pretty nose. He hastened to explain. "The numbers didn't cooperate, that's all. I'm sure next week will be better." He took a breath, then ventured forward. "Yours?"

The smile almost reached her eyes. "Did you send Doris after me again?"

"No. Should I have?"

"Maybe. She came and practically demanded I get dressed and follow her."

Art sucked in a breath. That could be bad, but Josie looked alive again. "Where did she take you?"

"To church." A soft chuckle slipped out. Art would have hugged plump Doris if she'd been in the room. A giggle from Josie! "She took me to help serve at its soup kitchen. I think I'd like to go back."

"Next week? That sounds fine." Especially if serving brought Josie back to him.

"No. Well, then, too. But Sunday. For services. Doris said we could walk with her." Her eyes begged him to say yes. "We haven't visited this one. Maybe it will be the right one for us."

"All right. If you want to try hers, we can. Sounds like a good church if they're meeting community needs."

Josie took his hand. "Thank you. I think we could meet some nice people there. Maybe Cincinnati will feel more like home." A wistful look took her away from him.

Squeezing her hand, Art cleared his throat. "Let's take a stroll. Enjoy the day." If they didn't hurry, evening would fall. "Before dinner." He pulled Josie to her feet. Her lips turned up at the corners as he tugged her to the door. He stopped, his breath disappearing in the face of her beauty. She might think she was broken, but he knew better. A strength she didn't recognize filled her.

Josie caught his stare. Softness removed the lines around her eyes. "I love you, Art Wilson." Before he could respond, she stood on tiptoe and stole the rest of his breath with a kiss.

He deepened the kiss, and thoughts of abandoning the walk played in his mind.

six

The alarm clock jangled on the bedside table, and Art jerked awake. He groped for the clock. After he silenced it, he lay toying with the idea of sleep. To make it to work on time, he needed to get up and move. Instead, he scooted closer to Josie. A sigh breathed from her lips as he pulled her close. She scooched nearer without opening her eyes.

For this moment, all was right in his world. He could pretend they hadn't lost the baby two months ago. And thank God, Josie was edging her way back to him, slowly returning to the same vibrant woman he'd married a few short months ago.

"Good morning, sweetheart."

A smile teased her face at his words. "Morning." She snuggled close a moment, then stretched. "Let me get you breakfast."

"Really?" He'd enjoy eating her eggs rather than his burnt toast.

She slipped out of bed and pulled on her robe. "I'll have it ready when you get out of the shower."

As he hurried through his morning preparations, the scent of bacon reached him. His stomach growled, and he laughed. Time to eat. When he reached the table, Josie had placed two plates of food on it. She sat at the table, Bible open in front of her as she waited.

"Find anything good?"

"Yes."

"I love seeing you like this."

She looked up at him, and her nose crinkled. "Like what?"

"Ready to tackle the day. It's been awhile."

"I know, and I'm sorry."

"I understand."

"Not really, but you try, and I appreciate that. Now I want you to enjoy your eggs." She turned to the stove and poured a mug of coffee before handing it to him.

Art mulled over her words, looking for hidden meaning. Could he address them, or should he leave them be? One thing he'd learned from watching his parents' tense relationship was to tread carefully where a woman's emotions were concerned. Scott had reinforced that lesson with his challenge. Art definitely didn't understand the depths of what moved those emotions. But each conversation helped.

She settled onto the chair next to his. He leaned over and kissed her cheek, pleased to watch a smile play across her lips. If he let himself linger there, he'd never get to work.

He grabbed his Bible. "Let's start a new practice in the mornings."

Josie looked at him, brows crunched. "Okay."

"I'd like to read a Bible passage with you each morning. We could start with Psalms. Spend a few moments connecting with each other and God before our days begin."

"I'd like that." A soft smile creased Josie's face.

ֵ

After devotions, he headed out the door. E. K. Fine's Piano Company had operated for decades without his daily presence, but at times, he wondered how. The books were finally falling into an order that delighted him.

The numbers marched across the books in even rows. And the timing couldn't be better.

Mr. Fine had directed the managers to find ways to turn the company's enterprises into militarily useful ventures.

Art's whistle echoed a bird's song as he ambled the blocks to the factory. His mom could tell him exactly which type of bird he echoed, but he had no idea other than the tune pleased him. His steps quickened to match the timing.

After winding through Eden Park, he reached the factory. He glanced up at the large clock tower in the center of the brick building. Five till nine. He'd arrived with a couple minutes to spare, but not as early as he'd hoped. Next time, he'd have to avoid whistling with the birds and get that head start on the day.

Even so, he didn't restrain the smile that tipped his mouth as he waltzed through the main doors. A turn to the left and then the right, and Art worked his way back to the office he shared.

Charlie Sloan looked up from the *Cincinnati Enquirer* spread across his desk. "Morning, Art."

"Morning." Art looked closer. The paper was too easy to read. Charlie had it upside down on his desk. "Good read?"

"Hmm?" Charlie looked down and grinned. "Practicing my upside-down reading skills."

Art laughed. "That's an unusual skill."

"But handy when one's called into Fine's office. The murmurs about the war keep me wondering. How many pianos do you think folks will buy then?"

"Not sure." He could only make an educated guess after working for the company only a few months.

"Not as many as you think. And I wouldn't be surprised if we're put on some kind of ration. I'm sure the government will have a better use for the materials we consume."

The coffee he'd had that morning burned through Art's stomach, leaving a horrible aftertaste in his mouth. Had this been a bad move? Wouldn't the new guy be the first to go if the company retreated?

"Don't let it worry you." Charlie patted a document on his desk. "Fine has a plan."

Art sank into his chair and faced the mountain of work. He tried to focus, but his thoughts circled back to Charlie's comments. What did he know about the piano industry? War seemed far off for the United States, but a few years ago, it had looked that way in Europe, too. What impact would entering the war have on an economy still recovering from the deep struggles of the last decade? God was in control. He knew that. But as the unspoken questions ricocheted off each other, he fought to cling to that truth.

His steps faltered as he left work that evening.

He'd made the right decision when he accepted the job and moved to Cincinnati. Despite everything happening, he believed that. God would watch over them, and even if the war somehow reached the United States, he'd have a job. The company would get creative, and he'd help with that if necessary.

His briefcase hung from his grip as he trudged up the steps to the apartment. They should have found one on a lower floor. Their third-floor apartment had too many steps to climb at the end of the day. He pushed his hat brim back and pushed onward. The aroma of something warm and chocolaty floated in the air. His stomach grumbled as he hoped it was brownies. If Josie had baked his favorite dessert, then she'd had a good day.

A door groaned as it opened. Sounded like his door. A tired grin tugged his face when Josie poked her head into the hallway. She wore a bright red dress that hugged her curves in all the right places. A fire to be close to her propelled him up the last steps.

"You are a sight for sore eyes."

A smug grin split her face at his words. "Glad to hear it. A man should want to come home to his wife at the end of the day." The words purred as they tickled his ear. Josie snuggled close, her head sliding perfectly under his chin, the puzzle piece that fit him.

He savored the moment. No matter what questions had pelted his mind, she was part of him.

A door squeaked below, and Josie pushed back. "Let's go inside. I don't want to give the Duncans a show."

"We are married, Josie."

She grimaced. "Still."

"All right." He let her pull him inside and shut the door. Tossing his briefcase to the side, he tucked her close again and inhaled the soft scent of something floral in her hair. Lavender? Maybe violets? Whatever it was, he'd have to keep her well stocked. "Did you bake me brownies?"

"Maybe. But first you have a telegram." She waved at an envelope sitting on the dining room table.

"Did you read it?"

"No, silly. It's addressed to you."

He chuckled. "We're married. You can read my mail."

"Remember that when you accuse me of invading your privacy." She crossed her arms and stared at the envelope.

"No worries about that." He picked up the envelope and slit it. Pulling out the sheet, he read the block letters once and then again:

8 YEAR OLD COMING *STOP* EVACUATING WITH
GROUP FROM LONDON *STOP* SHOULD ARRIVE EARLY
JULY *STOP* MORE DETAILS COMING *STOP* WINIFRED
WILSON

Josie read the words over Art's shoulder. Did the telegram really say someone planned to send a child? To them? An eight-year-old? In July? The calendar pages had already fluttered to May. Josie gulped as she looked at the words again. This child would arrive in two months. She worried her lower lip between her teeth as she considered how to fit a stranger's child into their apartment. It was comfortably cozy for two. Still, the spare room would have to transform into a bedroom.

Why would anyone send a child to them? Especially this Winifred Wilson, whoever she was?

A furrow had formed along the bridge of Art's nose as he read. He mouthed the words.

"What does it mean?" Josie took a deep breath and tried to push the shrillness from her voice. "Do you know Winifred?"

Art shook his head, a puzzled expression on his face. "I'm not sure. The name's vaguely familiar, but I can't place it. Guess I'll call Mom and get the scoop. She's probably a distant cousin looking for a safe place for her child to live during the war."

Josie rubbed her forehead, where a tight band gripped her. Germany had just invaded France and Belgium, so she could understand the desire to get a child away from the seemingly inevitable invasion of England. What would she do with an eight-year-old? There was no indication if the child was a boy or girl. The thought of a boy running all over the cramped space caused her to catch her breath.

"Do you realize this says the child will arrive by early July? This is May."

A frown creased Art's face as he watched her. "Maybe I should call Mom now."

That sounded like the best thing to do. Maybe she'd have more information. Josie wanted to be available, but the telegram didn't provide enough information.

Art headed downstairs to use the phone in the grocery store, and Josie trailed him. Mr. Duncan waved them over, and soon Art had dialed his parents' home. Josie crowded next to Art and picked at a fingernail while she waited for the conversation to start.

"Mom? Josie and I got a telegram today from Winifred Wilson. Do you know her?" Art nodded and hmmed a bit. "Really? A distant cousin. Do you know how she knew to get ahold of me? . . . Okay. . . She wants us to take their daughter in. From England." Art's brows bunched together as he listened. "Grandfather said that? All right. Have fun at your dinner."

Art hung up and looked at Josie. "Winifred is my third cousin." He shrugged. "Grandfather told her how to get ahold of us. Told her we were the young, vibrant couple that could keep up with her little girl. He's paying her way here."

"Really?" The man was a mystery to Josie.

"Well, I guess we wire back that we'll take the girl."

Josie drew in a deep breath and released it. She glanced around the small store. "I don't know where we'll put a child. . . or what we'd do with one. . .but we'll make it work. It won't be easy, though."

"Probably not, but it's the right thing to do."

Josie rubbed a hand across the ache hitting her head. Art was right, and ready or not, they'd soon be foster parents to an eight-year-old. Josie could only imagine the problems and challenges of a child removed from all he or she knew and loved.

seven

Days passed without any further information about the girl. Art's mom didn't know any more than she'd already told them, and no answer had come to Art's telegram that they would shelter the child as long as requested. Josie tired of looking around the apartment, wondering where a girl and her belongings would fit. The second bedroom seemed too small—little more than a closet, really—but it remained the only option.

The more Josie tried to imagine sending a child across an ocean to live on a continent with strangers, the more she wondered at the sacrificial love behind the act. One afternoon as she sat at the kitchen table reading her Bible, it struck her. It was an act of desperation. Desperation to provide for the well-being of a daughter. Desperation to ensure her safety.

In some ways, that act mirrored the despair Moses' mother must have felt when she set him in a basket of reeds and pushed him into the waters of the Nile with no idea or promise of the outcome—merely the knowledge death waited if she did nothing. The act would require such trust and sacrifice. Trust that God would intervene. And Jochebed's willingness to sacrifice her dreams of how life should be. All to save her son.

Josie wanted to welcome the child, not merely endure the intrusion. The stay could be too long to allow it to become simply a duty. It could actually be fun to have the girl join them. It would certainly fill days that bordered on purposeless now.

Summertime in Cincinnati. They could take the child to Cincinnati's amusement park, Coney Island, and to Reds baseball games. Maybe she'd save baseball for a time Kat visited. Kat could explain the game to their guest. Josie had never understood the rules—certainly not enough to make someone who may never have seen a game understand. Maybe Art would fill in those details.

Josie shook her head. There was so much about her husband she still didn't know. Fortunately, God had given her a lifetime to uncover all the details, the likes and dislikes. With another weekend upon them, maybe she should make a point to learn what she could. She could call it a treasure hunt. Search for the nuggets that made Art the man he was.

The mantel clock chimed a new hour. Five o'clock. Time to get ready for Art to come home. Josie hurried to the bathroom and pinched her cheeks before adding a touch of color to her lips. She whipped a brush through her hair and practiced her smile in the mirror. A glow filled her eyes that she wondered at. Her mom often got a soft, doe look around her eyes when thinking about Josie's dad. This was the first time Josie had noticed the same look in her eyes.

The clock eased toward five thirty, and restlessness propelled her out the door and down the stairs. She couldn't stand to wait another moment in the apartment. No, the day was beautiful enough to meet him on the sidewalk. A streetcar zipped down the middle of the street. She cupped a hand at her brow, shielding her eyes from the sun.

Josie scanned the sidewalk, looking for his familiar gait. There. Her breath caught at the sight of him walking her way. His shoulders were pushed back, hat thrust at a jaunty angle on his curls.

She knew the moment he saw her, because a big smile cracked his face and he picked up his pace.

"Josie." He picked her up and twirled her around right there on the sidewalk. "Ready for an evening out?"

She looked down at her plain skirt and simple white blouse. "That depends on where we're going."

"Get on your walking shoes, baby. We're headed to Coney Island."

Josie shrieked and held on tight. "That sounds perfect. But no roller coasters."

"You'll love them."

She wrinkled her nose and made a face. She couldn't imagine riding a roller coaster, even though she'd heard they could be fun.

Art laughed and patted her cheek. "Go on. You've got fifteen minutes to get ready."

"Yes, sir." She kissed him on the cheek, then spun and rushed inside.

A glow filled Josie at the thought of an evening exploring the amusement park. Even if it meant talking Art out of roller coasters. Moonlite Garden could be fun, too, since dancing had been one of the activities they'd enjoyed while courting, but in the months they'd been in town, they hadn't made it to Coney Island or other venues. The thought of finally visiting the amusement park and seeing the famous ballroom and oversized swimming pool excited her.

❧

Art watched as Josie pulled a navy dress out of the wardrobe. Its vibrant color accented the blooms on her cheeks. She looked in the mirror, fingers playing with her makeup doodads. He hoped she realized she didn't need anything to enhance her beauty. *Thank You, Lord, for this gift.* He had a feeling he would never tire of watching her or enjoying her. No, especially when life sparkled in her eyes for the first time in a while. While he hoped it wasn't merely the prospect of a night out, he'd enjoy it. But if a night out brought this response, he'd make sure he planned more.

Josie tucked a strand of hair behind her ear. "Ready?"

He'd been so engaged in watching her that he hadn't done anything else. Art cleared his throat. "All right. Need a wrap?"

"Just a sweater, please."

Art reached behind the door for where she stored them. He ran his hand along the four or five there. "Which?"

"This one." Josie brushed past him and smiled as it slid from the hook into her arms. The fabric felt like a caress. Maybe they should stay in. . . . Another look at her face and her excitement and he decided no. They'd explore the amusement park first. She pulled on her sweater, her face inches from his. She must have read something in his expressions, because a softness claimed her.

"Later." Promise filled the single soft word she breathed. He nodded. He could wait.

He tore his eyes from her mouth and gestured toward the door. "This way, milady."

The Packard served as their steed, and soon they arrived at Coney Island. The lights pulsed from the roller coasters even though it wasn't yet twilight. He couldn't wait to show Josie the sight when the rides stood against a dark sky.

They strolled arm in arm around the outskirts of the park past the Moonlite Gardens. The swinging sounds of "A-Tisket, A-Tasket" reached his ears. He laughed as Josie bopped in time to the music. "Maybe we'll take that in another night."

Her giggle sounded like music, made sweeter by its absence. She stepped closer to him. "The night is perfect just spending it with you."

"I hope you still think so when it's over."

"I will." She reached up, and he stopped. The air came alive with expectation. She leaned in and kissed him. "Thank you."

The wail of a saxophone pierced the air. "Come on. Let's see what rides this place has."

Josie willingly followed his lead as they strolled the park.

❧

They walked past a small Ferris wheel, lights lit as it spun round and round. Calypso music tinkled their way from the carousel. The animals rode up and down as it circled over and over. Art made a beeline for the roller coaster next to the carousel. The Wildcat stretched across the back of the park. Josie eyed its length. The ride towered above her, then rolled up and down in a pattern. Art bounced on his toes, and Josie steeled herself. She had to ride that beast. Surely it couldn't be any worse than riding a car through mountain passes. Who was she kidding? Josie gulped and pulled back.

"What?"

"I'm not sure I can ride that thing."

Art looked from her to the roller coaster. "Come on. It'll be great. You'll enjoy it so much I won't be able to get you off it."

Josie highly doubted that. A train rattled to a stop. The folks getting off had big grins stretched across their faces. None looked like they'd fared poorly because of the ride. "All right. I'll go, but we'd better do it now before I change my mind."

Art tugged her toward the line. Before she'd steeled herself, they were climbing into a car and buckling into the bench seat. Josie bit her lip as the car faltered in its steep climb. They crested the hill, and Josie's heart stopped. They towered above the city, and she could see the downtown skyline in the distance. The view was amazing, dotted with the twinkling lights of a city bathed in dusk.

"Maybe this isn't so bad."

"The ride's barely started." Art's words tickled her ear.

"Really?" Josie turned to him, then sucked in a breath as the train plummeted over the edge of the hill. The car jerked and pulled from side to side. Her teeth clacked together, and her knuckles whitened where she clung to the bar. She shut her eyes, but a scream still escaped. Art tugged her to him, and his chest vibrated with laughter. Josie peeked as the train eased its descent. Oh no! They were climbing another hill.

Finally, the ride ended, and they stumbled out of the car. Josie almost dropped to her knees to kiss the ground. "I've never been shaken so hard. People think that's fun?"

"Admit it—you enjoyed it."

"Maybe a tad."

He spun her away from him and grinned. "More than that."

Art looked longingly at the ride, then led Josie down the walkway. An easy silence fell as Josie watched other couples walk by hand-in-hand.

"What do you wish for?"

Josie stopped and turned toward him. What?

❧

Art smiled at Josie. The night was going so well. He couldn't wait to hear her answer. Josie's gaze drifted from him to some spot across the crowded floor. He tried to follow it but couldn't see what had captured her attention. "Let's sit down." Josie tugged him toward a park bench.

They worked their way through the crowd.

"So you haven't answered my question." He hoped she'd give him a glimpse into her heart. Where did her wishes and dreams lie?

She nodded, keeping her eyes fixed on the table. "Have you ever been afraid to wish for something? Afraid that if you speak it, the dream will die?"

"Not that I remember." Where was she headed with this thought?

Josie settled back as if somehow that simple sentence had told her everything she needed to know. "I really want to understand, Josie."

"It's nothing, really." Her mouth twisted as if the words had a bitter taste to them.

Art squeezed her hands and held on until she looked at him. "All I hope is your wishes include me. I only want to make you happy. Give you moments like this."

"I do love you, Art. My life is so much richer with you in it." She hesitated.

He opened his mouth to probe further into her dreams, but she rushed to speak before he could. "Someday we'll have children, and then I'll look back and long for these days when it was you and me." A shuttered look fell over her face.

"Are you afraid we might lose another child?" He hadn't considered that.

"It's silly, I know."

"No, I can understand. We'll have a family. At the right time. And then you'll wish for some relief." He leaned back and draped his arm around her shoulders. "I like that dream. Kids."

"Someday." A wistful smile touched her. He didn't know how to comfort her and felt like he had to treat her with kid gloves. "Until then," she added, "we'll serve God as best we can. Maybe take in your cousin."

"Those aren't dreams."

"It's enough for now. Living with you. Spending time together."

He almost believed her. But he also heard the cry of her heart, and he could do nothing about that. He wanted to live in this moment. Instead, the shadow of yesterday and the uncertainty of tomorrow hung between them.

Until someday arrived.

eight

Josie curled on the couch with a copy of *The Grapes of Wrath*. She set the copy to the side and stared out the window. Miss Adelaide had foisted it on her the last time she stopped at the library. While she'd enjoyed the movie, she struggled with the book so far. When the passing traffic served to hold her interest more than the book, there was a problem.

"Must be me." She shook her head and looked at the book. Maybe the lazy June heat prevented her from comprehending what she read. Josie reached behind her, pushing the lace curtain to the side. Not even the hint of a breeze slipped through the open window.

The thump of steps on the stairs pulled her from her drowsy state. A light knock beat a rhythm on the door. With a sigh, Josie pushed off the couch and walked to the door. "Yes?"

"Is this the residence of Mr. and Mrs. Wilson?" A voice that sounded overly cultured filtered through the door.

"Yes." Josie opened the door.

A slight woman dressed in a neatly tailored suit with a smart hat bobbing on top of her upsweep stood in front of her. The plaid of her suit matched the currently popular ones Josie had seen in catalogs. "I'm Miss Annabelle Rogers. Here to do a home visit in anticipation of you receiving a child."

A home visit for a child? What could the woman mean? Unless it had something to do with the unanswered telegram.

"May I come in?"

"Yes." Josie shook the woman's hand and invited her in. "I have to admit I'm confused about why you're here."

"May I?" Annabelle inclined her head toward the couch.

Warmth filled Josie's cheeks. Where were her manners?

61

"Of course. Would you like anything to drink?"

"Not now, thank you."

Josie sank into the armchair and studied the woman, who couldn't be much older than she was. She pulled files and a small notebook from a leather briefcase, setting them in a precise order next to her on the couch. Her nails were painted a rich red that matched her lips. And her face was pleasant though not beautiful. With her files arranged, she looked up with a tight smile.

"I've been hired by the families sending their children to the United States to ensure the homes are suitable for children."

Josie's back stiffened at the words. Not suitable? Of course, she and Art would make wonderful foster parents.

"You're one of a few families in Cincinnati. Most of my time will be spent in Canton." Josie's face must have reflected her confusion, because the woman rushed to continue. "The Hoover Company is arranging transit for almost one hundred of its employees' children."

"How does this impact us? Art's distant cousin asked us to take a child. We haven't heard anything since answering that we were willing, but surely they wouldn't ask if they didn't want us to have the child."

Annabelle's eyebrows raised, and she shook her head slightly. "You don't have children yet, do you?"

Josie swallowed as she tried to again decide how to answer the question. She did have a child. Just not here in her womb or arms.

"Once you do, you'll understand a parent's need to ensure those caring for their children are qualified." The woman opened a file and made some notations. "How long have you been married?"

The questions spilled on top of each other until Josie felt drained. Annabelle finally asked for a tour of the space. She continued to make notations, leaving Josie exposed. If only she'd had notice and the opportunity to clean. She cringed each time she noticed a cobweb or a dust bunny. Would they not receive this child all because every surface didn't sparkle? She couldn't let the child down like that.

Finally, the woman collected her files and smiled her smug, slightly superior smile. "That should be all. Thank you for your time."

"Is there anything else we need to do?"

"Once I've met your husband, we should be done, unless I have additional questions."

"It shouldn't be a problem to meet Art. We'll get a time from you? When will we learn the date the girl arrives? Do you know anything about her?"

"The children are scheduled to journey over in July. I will meet the group and chaperones in New York and journey with them to Ohio. If Cassandra Wilson's parents agree you are suitable, you can expect to have her join you within six weeks. Time is critical in getting the children away from the war."

Josie nodded. She couldn't imagine not having the child, Cassandra, join them. Sometime during the last hours, she had fully committed herself to welcoming this child. So their lives would need some adjustment. Everything worth doing required a sacrifice. And if they could ease the child's life for a period, so much the better.

"Will you be of assistance once the child arrives?" She cleared her throat. "Once Cassandra joins us?"

"Yes. I'll have ongoing site visits and be available to answer questions. You won't be left alone to figure out what to do." Now that the interview had concluded, it was as if a layer of ice had slid from Annabelle. "I will do my best to ensure that the match is successful for the duration."

"Thank you." Josie stood at the door after Annabelle left. Soon Cassandra would join them. She looked around the room, seeing a thousand items to take care of before then.

&

Art fought the urge to laugh as Josie spun around the rooms in her perpetual motion that hadn't eased since Annabelle

Rogers visited a week earlier. She flitted near him, and he pulled her into his lap.

"Here, rest a moment. You'll wear yourself out before another day passes. You need to reserve some energy for the child, you know."

She pouted, lips puckered but sparks in her eyes. "I know. But I refuse to leave one thing for that Annabelle to find fault with. I can tell she'll be a hard taskmaster."

"I thought you said she warmed to you."

"Yes." She drew the word out to several syllables. "But I won't make it easy for her to mark us down on her forms."

He chucked her under her chin. "Maybe she's writing us up."

"Maybe. But I don't think so."

"Well, you've made the decision easy for me. Pack an overnight bag. First thing in the morning, we'll load the Packard and head home for the weekend."

Her shriek left him rubbing his ear, hoping he'd hear in the morning.

"You mean it?" He nodded as she squealed again. "It will be wonderful to go home."

"Then we will. Who knows when we'll get away again once Cassandra arrives."

Her kiss was all he needed to know the suggestion was perfect. It would be good to visit family, maybe see some friends.

The next morning, they were up early, Josie pushing to get them on the road. The Packard carried them down the highway. With the windows rolled down, the breeze ruffled Josie's hair and kept the heat from stifling the car. The miles ticked by until they finally pulled into Dayton. Art wound through the southern neighborhoods until they neared the area surrounding the University of Dayton.

Josie's family's home nestled on Volusia Avenue south of the university, where her father taught. Stately trees lined the street where the homes had yards unlike even a couple blocks away where the houses practically touched each other. As he parked, Art braced himself for the barrage that was sure to come. Her family moved at a different pace than his and seemed to have only one gear: fast and loud.

"Oh, I hope they haven't left already." Josie leaned out the window and bounced as she waited for him to open her door.

He rolled his eyes. "It's only eleven. I don't think you have to worry about that."

"You don't know us very well yet." The use of *us* was softened only slightly by the smile on her face. She wasn't part of that *us* anymore. He was supposed to be her only family. He opened the door, and Josie accepted his hand, giving him a dazzling smile in the process. Maybe he'd overlook her words. She didn't really mean them. "Come on, slowpoke."

Josie rushed through the front door as if she'd never moved into her own home. "I'm home. Mom? Dad?"

A squeal that could only come from her kid sister split the air. "Josie." Clomping feet indicated Kat barreled their way. She was dressed in a baseball uniform and almost knocked Josie down when she barreled into her. "You're here." After a quick hug, she slugged Josie in the shoulder. "Why'd you stay away so long? Did you get married or something?"

Josie giggled and locked arms with Kat. "Do you have a game today? Can we come?"

"Sure. But we have to leave soon. Dad's taking me since Mark says he has to study." The look on Kat's face communicated she didn't believe him. "You'd think he'd want to come."

"Let us come instead. We'd love to. Right, Art?"

He tried to look eager at the chance to sit in the hot sun and watch kids play ball. If he were going to watch ball, he'd rather it be the Reds. But if it would keep Josie happy, he'd do it. He'd take a magazine with him. After all, how well could girls play?

Josie's mom hurried out of the kitchen. A large apron was tied around her waist, but flour dotted her sleeves and face. "Josie." She pulled her daughter into a hug and whispered something in her ear. Josie nodded.

"I'm so sorry about the baby. Are you sure you're okay?"

Josie nodded. "I'm fine, though there are days."

"We're still praying for you." Mom stepped back. "Let's get you a quick bite before the game."

Art and Josie joined Mr. Miller at the game. The team turned out to be co-ed, thanks to Kat's presence, and Art had to admit that for a girl, and a young one, she played well.

"Where'd she learn?"

"Mark. I think that's why she's hurt he won't come to her games."

"How many does she play in a week?"

"At least two if it's anything like prior summers."

Art shook his head. This girl was unlike others he knew. To be that committed to a man's game. Why hadn't Mr. Miller talked to her about the need to act like a lady? She was approaching fourteen and playing with men after all.

"I'm glad our girls won't do things like that." The words must have left his mind via his mouth because Josie turned on him.

"I would hope that any child of ours who wanted to participate in physical activity would have the chance. If that means organized teams, what of it? You have to admit Kat is good."

She was. And there lay the problem. Some things girls didn't do. Some things were sacred to men.

But he'd never seen anything like Kat nabbing a pop fly and the young men rallying around her.

Saturday passed in a blur with Josie's family. The warmth was a welcome change from the formal atmosphere with his family. While he might not be sure about the ball playing, he enjoyed the other competition in the family. He and Mark locked wits over a game of chess that left Art scrambling for the advantage.

Sunday lunch with his family was another story. During the formal meal, the clink of silver on china served as the musical backdrop to an awkward silence. Art tried to enjoy his beef Wellington but couldn't as he noticed Josie tense. When Grandfather invited him to his study, Art knew it wasn't for a casual conversation, but couldn't imagine why Grandfather would summon him since he'd ignored them both during the meal.

"Would you like a drink?" Grandfather approached a small cabinet behind his desk and arched an eyebrow at Art.

"No, sir."

"Still a teetotaler I see."

"Just chose not to drink."

"All right." Grandfather settled in his leather chair behind his massive desk. "So, boy, how's business in Cincinnati?"

Art sipped his beverage and sighed. So it began. "Fine. My employer's trying to anticipate what will happen if we enter the war."

"Tell him not to waste his time. We won't enter. If we did, we'd never recover. Your mother tells me you're taking in one of the British cousins."

"We've been asked to."

"Glad to hear it. Wonder what would make the parents consider you rather than some of the more established relations."

"Mom said you suggested it."

A twinkle filled his grandfather's eyes. "So I did. Delighted you've decided to accept her."

"We're happy to help. Actually, excited about it."

"Harrumph. Don't know that there's anything to be excited about, since I doubt they can pay anything."

"They don't need to."

"Tell me that after you've provided food and clothing for a child." Grandfather shook his head, then took out his cigar box. He selected a cigar and shoved it between his teeth without lighting it. "Mark my words: you'll need help."

"What would you have us do? Leave her in danger when they've asked for our help?"

"No, but watch your pennies. I'm willing to help some, but

your grandmother and I won't underwrite her entire stay. In that case, we might as well keep her here."

"That won't be necessary, sir."

"Keep it in mind."

"Yes, sir."

The conversation wandered from there. Grandfather probed him about the company and mood of Cincinnati. By the time they left, Art's mind had wearied of the grilling, and he was relieved to leave the family estate behind and take the highway toward Cincinnati.

nine

Josie dusted a corner of the knick-knack table in the living room. She turned to another surface, but there was nothing to dust. Every surface had been wiped and scrubbed for days.

Her heart sank, and she lowered herself to the couch. They'd only been home a week, but she felt odd. Mark went to school. While she wouldn't want his homework—he had a crazy amount as an engineering student—she would like the direction he had. And Kat lived life with an energy that left Josie longing for a fraction of it. Even Carolynn, her best friend, seemed to have moved on with a verve that left Josie wondering if her presence had mattered when she lived in Dayton.

Everyone seemed fine without her.

Why couldn't she say the same?

Enough moping. She pulled on shoes, grabbed her purse, and headed out the door. The June sun beat down on her, and she wished she'd grabbed a hat to shade her eyes. Instead of going back upstairs to get one, she waved at Mr. Duncan as he swept the sidewalk in front of the store. With a quick glance for traffic, she ran up McMillan Street toward the library. When she reached it a few minutes later, she hesitated. Why had she come? She didn't need any books, since the few she had needed to be read.

"Come in, dear." She must have hesitated at the door too long since Miss Adelaide had come to her. "I hoped I'd see you today."

"You did?"

"Wanted to talk to you about something. In out of the sunshine first. Can't leave the desk too long, you know." Miss Adelaide shooed her inside, returned to her seat, and smiled in satisfaction. "There now."

"How can I help you?" Josie leaned against the desk.

"I'll be taking a vacation this summer, and I need someone to mind the branch." Miss Adelaide focused on Josie, while Josie's mind rushed in confusion. Why tell her this? "My favorite niece is expecting her first child. There's no way that event can happen without me. There's just one problem."

"There is?"

"Yes. Who will mind the library? The young lady who sometimes fills in for me has left town herself for the summer. And the student who works in the evenings isn't interested in working from nine to nine all summer."

"Surely someone from one of the other branches will step in."

Miss Adelaide's lips curved down. "They could. But they never come here. They don't have a clue where things are or how we like them done."

"Don't all the branches use the Dewey system?"

"That's not what I mean, and you know it, Josie. No need to get impertinent."

Josie struggled to keep her face placid. No need to add to Miss Adelaide's indignation. "So why tell me?"

"Why, you will take my place while I'm gone." Miss Adelaide said the words as if they were clear to anyone with any sense.

"Me? I have no training."

"Maybe. But you love books, you know the library, and you're my choice." Standing with her arms crossed and a stern look on her face, Miss Adelaide looked like she believed she could force her will.

Josie sighed. "We'll have a little girl joining us in the next month. I don't know that I can care for her and do something like this."

"Bring her with you."

"I don't know that it's that simple. I'm sure she'll want to do other things." And what would Art think?

"Well, you're my choice. Talk to your husband and let me

know if you can do it in the next week."

Almost against her will, Josie nodded. Miss Adelaide might be small, but she had a forceful personality. "Let me look for a book."

Miss Adelaide turned to help a patron without giving Josie another look. As Josie wandered the stacks, the idea grew on her. It could be a nice outlet for a few weeks. And surely Cassandra would like the library. What girl wouldn't?

The evening passed slowly. Josie left supper warming in the oven as she waited for Art. The clock hands moved around its face while she waited. She picked up several books but couldn't escape into any. By the time he made it home after nine, she couldn't talk to him about anything. If she didn't know better, she'd say there was smoke clinging to him. But he didn't smoke.

He'd scarfed down his dinner, then settled on the couch with a paper.

"What kept you late tonight?"

He didn't even look up. "A project, then out with a couple guys afterward."

"I missed you."

"They've been after me for months, so I thought now would be a decent time before Cassandra arrives." The paper slid down so that she could see his face. "I assumed it would be okay."

Josie nodded. "It's fine. I just wondered."

❧

Later the next morning, Doris slipped into the apartment, bringing the sweet smell of muffins with her.

Josie smiled when she saw the basket on Doris's arm. "You must think I never eat."

"You are on the thin side." She patted Josie as she brushed by. "I hope Art likes you that way. Scott likes me with a little more padding." Doris worked around the kitchen as if it was her own. "I've got Bible study in an hour. You should come."

Josie tensed. "I won't have anything in common with anyone."

"You don't know that. You bemoan not having friends here, but I don't see you do anything about it." Her eyes narrowed as she crossed her arms. "Time to quit whining and act. Besides, you won't have any of these muffins unless you join me."

"Then what are you doing?"

"Teasing you with the scent and getting your coffee ready. You don't have much time."

Josie considered fighting Doris, but one look convinced her the only outcome was to give in with grace. "All right. When do I need to be ready?"

"Fifteen minutes," Doris stated matter-of-factly as if it was the most natural thing in the world to walk into someone's home and demand they do something.

Josie shook her head and hurried to her room.

An hour later, she followed Doris into the fellowship room of the church. Several knots of women gathered around the outskirts of the room or in chairs. While she and Art had attended a few Sundays with the Duncans, Josie didn't know any of the women. Several glanced their way, but Doris led her to the coffee table. Setting her basket on the table, she pulled back the towel. The women quickly gathered.

"Are those your famous cinnamon muffins, Doris?" A tall redhead slipped between them.

"Yes they are, Rita. Would you like one?"

"Yes, ma'am. I'd like more, but will have one." She patted her tummy. "Still working on the baby."

Josie considered her, then shook her head. "You look wonderful."

"Tell that to Joey." She sighed dramatically. "It's been a year, and I have a couple pounds left. As long as Doris keeps bringing her treats, I think they'll be permanent residents." She winked at Doris. "Not that I mind." She took a bite of the muffin, bliss settling on her face. "Yes, ma'am, these are delectable." She startled. "Good heavens, I'm being a terrible hostess. My name's Rita Brown. You are. . . ?" Rita extended a slender hand to Josie.

"Josephine Wilson, but my friends call me Josie."

"Josie it is." A woman stood up across the room and clapped her hands. Rita leaned close. "That's the signal. Subtle, isn't it?"

Josie stifled a giggle with her hand. Maybe this wouldn't be so bad after all. But as the women discussed 1 Samuel 1, she reevaluated. Many of the women were Doris's age or older. In all likelihood equally sweet, but not people she immediately connected with. She didn't want a grandma telling her what to do. She wanted a friend who would laugh and cry with her. But many of the younger women were mothers with small children. Even though she enjoyed Rita, pain pierced her heart each time she saw Rita's little girl. By now, her own stomach would have been firmly rounded, and no one would question her state.

It didn't help that the scripture focused on Hannah and her desperate pleas for a child. Josie wondered if she'd ever understand why God allowed the things He did. Why could some women so easily have children, while others remained barren and desperately longing for a babe? Still other children suffered from illness or died at young ages.

She must have sighed out loud, for Rita patted her hand. She leaned close. "You all right, Josie?"

Josie sniffed and nodded. Doris leaned across Josie toward Rita. "This is a hard topic for the girl."

The leader sent pointed looks their way, but Doris and Rita continued to talk over Josie. Josie shrugged an apology to the woman. It wasn't her fault that the lesson hit so close to her heart. Or that her neighbors had decided now was the time to discuss her. She elbowed Doris and frowned.

Doris winked at her and went back to talking about Josie as if she weren't there.

Josie tried to ignore them, but a thought kept flashing through her mind. What if Doris had insisted she come today because of the topic? What if she'd decided Josie needed more than a new forum to meet people? A swirl of emotions played through her at the thought she'd been manipulated. She tried to pull her thoughts back to the passage, but each time she did, another pang went through her.

A woman across the circle wiped moisture from her face. What caused her tears? Had she lost a child, or was she unable to have one? Josie felt pressure build in her nose as she imagined the woman's story. Pain welled up, and she forced back tears that weren't focused on her own loss.

This was crazy! She had enough to handle without adding another's pain to her own. She should get up and leave. Let Doris explain for her. Instead, she pushed her chair back and read the passage.

Hannah had begged for children, longed for them, made vows to God to obtain them. And God eventually heard her. Then He allowed her to have Samuel. The praises overflowed from her heart.

Josie had not longed for children with such a passion. Until she had lost this child, it had been a distant idea, something that would occur in the future. As the conversation swirled around her, she lowered her head.

Father, help me seek Your face in the midst of this. I don't want to forget this life I lost, but I also don't want to linger in the grief. Help me move forward. Bring me to a place that I can rejoice in You again. Not because of what You might give me. Not to entice You to grant my requests. But praise You because of who You are.

Tears streamed down her cheeks as peace filled her heart. For a moment, it seemed God had come down and danced over her. She soaked in His presence, desperate to memorize it. She didn't know how long it would last, but she wanted to capture the feeling for the hard days that would come.

God hadn't forgotten her.

ten

The noise ricocheted off the ceiling as the men entered Rosie's, the neighborhood establishment. Stan swaggered as if he'd returned home from a long absence. Art grimaced. As far as he knew, that's how Stan felt. Art shouldn't be here. Calling it an establishment did not hide its true nature. While he might drink a Coke, everyone else ordered beers. Why had he allowed Stan to talk him into venturing out with the other guys again? This simply wasn't something he enjoyed.

And if Josie found out. . .

The thought lingered. What would she think? He didn't know, but he assumed she wouldn't be pleased.

He rubbed the back of his neck, felt the prickly hairs. Time to get a haircut. Hadn't he seen a barber down the street? He could still leave and get the haircut taken care of rather than stay with the guys. As he prepared to push off the barstool, the bartender set a mug in front of him. Foam sloshed over the sides. Who would have ordered him a beer?

"Bottoms up." Stan leered at him over the top of a matching mug.

Art scowled. His father had preached the lesson loud and clear. Only fools who couldn't control themselves visited those places. Drinking should be done within the walls of a man's home. Art shook the image from his head.

"Come on, time to loosen up. You're too uptight, even if you are a bean counter."

"Aw, leave him alone, Stan." George Brothers peered behind him, scanning the room.

"Find what you're looking for?" Stan's disgust was clear. "You know she ain't interested in you."

"Sure she is. She just needs to know me."

Unease set up camp in Art's core. He didn't know who they were talking about, and he didn't want to. He needed to leave. Now. These two fancied themselves a regular Abbott and Costello. First problem? They missed the speedy humor of skits like "Who's on First." Second problem? He couldn't believe he was listening to their vulgar comments.

Stan sat at one side of him, George on the other. Art ran his hands along the top of the long bar. It wasn't smooth as he'd thought. Instead, the wood was dented and battered. His thoughts raced as he looked for a way out.

Okay. So this wouldn't be easy. He should have never agreed to join them a couple weeks ago. When had it become easier and easier to walk in?

He glanced at his watch. Six thirty. Josie wouldn't be happy. She'd noticed his other absences. While she hadn't said anything, he knew that would change. Hopefully, this was one of the days she'd spent time at the library shadowing Adelaide. She might not even notice he was late. "I've got to leave." He threw some change on the bar and stood. "See you next week."

Traffic blared around him as Art double-timed it home. He barely noticed when he almost stepped into the path of a cab. His thoughts remained fogged. He needed to have his head examined. Choosing to spend more time with those guys rather than rush home to his bride. He knew better than to let Grandfather's disapproval settle into his spirit.

Friday night. They had the weekend to spend together. Thankfully, tonight was free.

&

Josie stared at Annabelle Rogers. Where was Art? She'd reminded him this morning the social worker would stop by for a last home visit before leaving to meet the children on the East Coast. He had to be here. It was the remaining step in satisfying Annabelle that Cassandra would thrive with them.

She picked at a fingernail. "Are you sure you wouldn't like something to drink?"

"No. This should be a quick visit." Annabelle cast a pointed look at her watch.

"He really should arrive any time." Josie hoped her words were true. Lately, Art hadn't rushed home. She didn't know what he did and wanted to avoid being the wife who nagged her husband about his whereabouts every day. Either she trusted him or she didn't. As long as she could, she'd choose trust. Believe the best about him. They'd exchanged promises, and she intended to keep hers.

She tried to make small talk, but the longer they waited, the more difficult the task. Annabelle didn't help things, either.

"I really must leave."

Josie grimaced. "I'm sorry you made the trip for nothing."

"Do you understand that we're out of time?" Her face pinched. "I'm not sure what to tell her parents. I can't vouch for your husband or his character."

"He's definitely a character." Josie smiled but realized Annabelle was too upset to take her words lightly. She cleared her throat. "He's wanted to host Cassandra from the moment we got the telegram."

"Then he should have been here to make sure we completed the paperwork." Annabelle stood and smoothed her skirt. "I may come by Monday night if he will be here."

"He will if I have to go get him myself." Josie followed her to the door. "Again, I'm sorry."

Annabelle strode past her and hurried down the steps. Josie eased the door shut. Everything in her wanted to slam it, but why worry Doris or risk the door? Art would be home soon, and then they'd figure out what was going on.

She paced the living room as she waited, gnawing on a nail. This wasn't like Art. Her heel caught the edge of the rug, and she sprawled against the couch. Her temper flared at the thought of the position he'd placed her in. He'd promised to be home. He'd understood he was required for the home visit. Maybe he'd changed his mind about Cassandra. Argh. She needed to talk to him. Understand what he was thinking. Trying to figure it out made her stomach clench.

Art sneaked through the door, as if he thought he could avoid her or she wouldn't notice his late arrival. He froze when he saw her sitting on the couch with her arms crossed. She bit her tongue to keep from saying something she'd regret.

A sheepish look filled his face. "Hi."

She nodded.

"I take it you missed me?" He tried to charm her with his Clark Gable smile.

She refused to soften. At least until he knew what he'd missed. "You're late."

"Yeah."

"Did you forget the appointment this evening?"

The color drained from his face. "The social worker?"

"Yes. She waited quite awhile but had to leave half an hour ago. Especially since I couldn't give her any indication of when you'd arrive."

He sank to the sofa next to her, then raked his hands through his hair. "I'm sorry, Josie."

"We may not get Cassandra now." How that thought pained her.

"She's not ours."

"But we're supposed to provide a safe haven for her. We can't do that until this home study is complete. And that won't happen unless Annabelle meets you." She sniffed the air. It was smoky but not the rustic aroma of wood smoke. "What did you bring home with you? Maybe it's a good thing you didn't meet. You smell like a bar."

He wouldn't meet her gaze. "Why? Why would you start going to bars now?"

"I don't."

She tried to scorch him with her stare.

"Okay, I have a couple times. But I'm not drinking, Josie. I promise."

Could she believe him? She had never imagined that was an option with him. And why now? Had she done something to push him away? She popped off the couch as her thoughts ran wild.

"Josie, calm down. You're acting crazy."

"I'm acting crazy? I'm only trying to make sure we can help your cousin. That's what you wanted. Did something change and you forgot to mention it?" Josie took a deep breath. If her voice got any louder, Doris and the grocer would hear every word.

Art hesitated. Had he changed his mind while she'd fallen in love with the idea of helping the girl?

"My job is getting intense. And you'll be working at the library this summer."

"You said it was okay."

"Sure, I did. It's clear you need an excuse to get out of the apartment and meet people." Art shrugged. "It seemed like a good way to help that happen. It's a lot with taking in a girl we don't know."

Josie gritted her teeth. "It will be fine. And this is a little late to change course. They leave in a couple weeks."

"We shouldn't force this. That's all I'm saying." Art crossed his arms and leaned against the couch. "Maybe I got too excited. Knight in shining armor and all that."

"How's that wrong? We all need a knight to save us from time to time."

"Maybe I'm not knight material." Art looked at his hands, and his voice cracked.

"Why say that?" Josie wrinkled her brow. "You're my knight."

"No. You keep looking at me like I'll fail."

If his eyes weren't dull with pain, Josie would have argued with him. But the longer she looked at him, the more she understood he really believed that. Somewhere, she had gone wrong in the months since they'd married. How could she restore him to his steed?

"Is that why you've stopped coming home after work?"

He hunched over, elbows on knees. The silence grew until Josie didn't know how to break it.

"It's been a hard week. Pressure from work. Trying to ignore Grandfather's voice in my head telling me that I have to work harder than the others and make my way in the world in a way that honors our family name. I honestly forgot, Josie. I didn't do it on purpose." He searched the room as if looking for more words. "I'm sorry, but that's all I can say."

"I'm sorry." Josie searched his eyes, then took a breath. "I hated not knowing where you were or what to do. If you don't want to take Cassandra in, I'll accept your judgment." Somehow she would make her heart agree.

"No, I'll call Miss Rogers and apologize. This is the right thing to do."

Josie tried to stretch her lips into a smile. Their conversation hadn't addressed the bars, but it was enough for now. At least he hadn't been drinking. Though how long could that last? And with an extra body to clothe and feed, there wouldn't be much left over for vices like that.

Art stood and pulled her toward him. She relaxed into him. They would make it through this and much more. The miscommunication would be fixed, and then Cassandra would be on her way.

eleven

Art paced the train depot's platform, his nervous energy wearing on Josie.

"Can you believe we're picking Cassie up today?"

"Um-hm." She'd spent the last two weeks getting the apartment ready. Once Art and Annabelle had talked, things had moved so quickly she was still spinning.

She pulled at her glove to see her watch, then scanned the horizon. Any time now the train should chug into the station, and she'd be a parent. The thought still seemed surreal. Earlier this year, she'd been unsure about having a baby; now she welcomed an eight-year-old.

But when a distant relative asked one to take in a child who was threatened by war, yes was the only correct answer. Who could have foreseen the turn the war would take? That evacuations abandoned last year would restart with the intensified air raids in London? That a relative would search hard enough to find Art?

Josie pulled off a glove and nibbled on a fingernail. Her nerves jumped with each sound.

Annabelle and Art had finally connected over lunch. Josie hadn't participated so hadn't told the social worker she'd taken a temporary job. All that mattered was that after a long lunch, Annabelle had given her approval to the match.

Just like that, they were on their way to pseudo-parenting.

Her stomach gurgled, and she pressed her hand firmly into it. Eight. Old enough to have fun and not require the close care of a smaller child. But also old enough to understand why she'd been sent from home. Josie remembered the abandonment she'd felt when left with her grandparents for a week. This was so much more than that. Could an eight-year-old truly grasp why parents sent them away? Not as punishment, but for protection? The choice must agonize.

Josie prayed they'd get along well. They had to since there was no end to this placement. She pulled in a shuddering breath. She must get her emotions under control before she let fear run away with her. Kat wasn't much older, and she'd see something like this as a grand adventure. Surely Cassandra would, too.

"Are you ready, honey?" Art stopped in front of her and grabbed her hands, running his fingers along her jagged nails.

She tried to smile but felt it quiver on the edges.

"Chin up. This will be great."

"I know."

"This is what you've worked so hard for. Helping this little girl."

"I don't know how little she'll be."

Art scooped her up and spun her around until she giggled.

"Put me down before I can't stand." Josie relaxed, grateful for Art's distraction. There was no reason to get so tense. This was what she wanted, after all.

Art resumed his pacing. "Why isn't the train here?"

"Soon enough."

A shrill whistle pierced the air. Art stopped his pacing and turned toward her, a grin splitting his face. The man certainly saw this as an escapade or some grand adventure.

"That's got to be her train."

Josie smiled as the beginning pushes of excitement vied with her questions What would this child add to their lives? "I'm sure it is."

"I wonder how we'll know her." From his jacket breast pocket he pulled a faded photo that Annabelle had provided. "Surely this isn't how she still looks."

Josie studied the pose again to amuse him. The girl with golden hair hanging in Shirley Temple curls looked about five, freckles dotting her nose above a charming grin. "No. But I don't think it will be hard to find her. How many little girls travel such distances? Her escort will surely look for us as we search for them."

The iron behemoth groaned and squealed as it slowed to a stop. Josie stepped forward and hooked her arm through Art's. "I'm excited to meet your cousin and welcome her."

Art's eyes shone with light. "That makes two of us. Here's hoping we don't overwhelm her."

People hopped off the train, some rushing into the arms of waiting loved ones, others striding into the terminal and out of sight at the clip of people with a mission. Josie scanned the dwindling crowd for two figures wandering, hunting for a contact.

"That must be her." The excitement in Art's voice mirrored his bouncing action. Josie grabbed her hat to keep it from sliding off and turned her gaze to where he pointed. Across the platform, a young girl walked in their direction, carrying a duffel and a lost look. Annabelle walked next to the child, a harried expression on her face and her clothes disheveled and wrinkled. What had happened on the train to leave Annabelle in such a state?

Josie took a step toward the child, unsure how best to approach her. Would the child welcome a hug, or would she find it invasive? Josie should have asked Annabelle such key questions before this moment. Now all she could do was look at Annabelle with a question in her eyes. Annabelle shrugged, exhaustion pushing her shoulders forward.

A whistle sounded, and the child jumped. She dropped the bag, and her sweet face pinched. Josie's heart tightened. This child had lived through things Josie hoped never to see or experience. She let go of Art and hurried to the child's side.

"Cassandra?"

The girl stood still, but a tear slipped down her cheek. Josie knelt in front of her, not caring if her own hose ripped with the movement.

"My name is Josie Wilson. You're going to live with us awhile." She touched the side of the girl's head and then lightly stroked her cheek. Only then did Cassandra stir. "Can we help you with your bag?"

Cassandra looked at her, face tinged red and eyes wide. "Sorry, ma'am." Her voice threaded the space between them in a whisper. "Will I live with you then?"

"Yes. We're delighted to have you live with us for a bit."

A wary knowing crept across Cassandra's face. "It's likely to be longer than that."

"Then you'll stay the duration. I promise."

Cassandra considered her a moment. Annabelle nudged her forward. "I hate to do this, but now that you're connected, I must get back on the train. There's one more soul to deposit with his new home. More miles to travel."

Art shook her hand. "Thanks for getting her safely here."

Annabelle nodded, then turned and hurried back to the train. Cassandra watched, a forlorn look shadowing her face. Time to distract her from another lost connection.

"Here. Let me introduce you to my husband, your cousin Art. Then we'll take you home, show you your room, have dinner, get you a bath." Josie bit her lip to stop the flow of words. "Sorry about that. I tend to talk when I'm excited."

"Any other time, too." Art laughed. "You'll be hard pressed to get a word in edgewise. Cassandra, I'm Art."

Cassandra looked at his hand and then shook it. She was small, wiry. Freckles on her small nose dotted strawberries-and-cream skin.

"A pleasure, sir." She laughed, but it sounded strangled and way too mature for a child. "Thanks for taking me."

"Did you enjoy your trip?" Art walked her toward the exit, her bag thrown over his shoulder.

"Once we were off the boat. We had to wear our life vests all the time, and I didn't like it."

"I see. Did you travel with many children?"

Cassandra shrugged, her thin shoulders poking through her dress. "Most of them went to a place called Canton. Do you know where that is? Miss Rogers said she needs to go there after she delivers Bobby. A company is taking those kids in."

"Will you miss the kids?"

Cassandra shrugged. "I didn't really know any of them before the trip."

"Would you like to see them again?"

"Maybe." A door seemed to shut in her expression.

"The first order of business is to get you an ice cream. All brave children need a treat." He led the child to the car, and Josie followed a small distance behind. The image of Art helping a little girl that looked like the best of both of them flashed through her mind. Someday. She smiled at the thought and the fact that the pain didn't accompany it. Maybe Cassandra was exactly what Josie needed to finish healing and stop dwelling on her own pain.

Cassandra nodded off in the car before they reached the drug store, so Art turned the car home instead. The moment they parked, Doris came running out the back doorway.

"You've arrived." She watched Art struggle to pull a sleeping Cassandra from the backseat. "Poor child must be all done in."

Josie nodded. "You would be, too, if forced to travel for weeks into the unknown."

"Well, you have the girl now and can befriend her."

The thought stilled Josie. She'd focused so much on getting Cassandra here that she hadn't considered the fact they were total strangers to the girl. While she'd worked hard to make the way for Cassandra, the child didn't know this.

Art groaned. "Could you close the car door, Josie? I'll get her upstairs."

"Here, let me get the back door for you." Doris chased Art across the backyard.

Josie closed the door, then leaned against the car. *Father, prepare my heart to be sensitive to the needs of this child You've sent our way. Give me insights into her, and help me be her friend. Help me remember she already has a mother.* Such sacrificial love left her blinking in the sunlight.

A window on the third floor opened. Art hung out and waved to her. "Coming, Josie?"

≥≥

It took several days to get Cassandra acclimated enough to willingly venture out. It seemed the child had brought the war with her. At loud, sudden sounds, she might dive for cover. Under a bed, under a table, the location didn't matter as long as she felt protected. The behavior charmed Josie at first but grew odd as Cassandra repeated it. Then Cassandra explained the air raid drills. The drills had been consistent but random. Josie prayed that Cassandra would reach a point where she didn't live life poised to hide at a moment's notice.

Josie also struggled to find foods that Cassandra liked. So many things Cassandra asked for sounded nasty, like haggis. Josie hadn't considered the conflict of the different cultures. The British spoke English, after all, but the differences highlighted the early days with their visitor.

A week after Cassandra arrived, they walked to the library branch. Josie needed to get Cassandra out of the house and prayed the sunshine would bring some life to the child. As Cassandra raced ahead, Josie decided this was what the child had needed.

"Cassandra, wait." Josie paused until the bounding child obeyed. While the neighborhood traffic stayed light during the day, cars zipped down the streets. She could just imagine the wire they'd have to send if something happened to Cassandra. SORRY *STOP* CHILD FLATTENED BY VEHICLE. She shuddered at the thought.

Cassandra skidded to a halt and smiled.

"I think you like the outdoors, Cassandra."

"It's much nicer here than in the city."

Josie laughed. "Your city is larger than this one. We'll have to explore some of the parks around here. Get you out more often."

Cassandra grinned at her and grabbed Josie's hand. She

swung it back and forth in large arcs until they reached the library. Once there, Cassandra raced up the steps and flung open the door. In a minute, she'd selected three books at random and stood at the checkout table, ready to leave. So much for a quiet time scanning the stacks for a few good reads.

"Can we leave now?" Cassandra's voice ricocheted off the ceiling and walls.

Miss Adelaide leaned forward, lips twisted in a mock frown. "Keep your voice down, young lady. You are in a library and should speak in subdued tones."

"Like this?" Cassandra whispered the words.

"Yes."

"All right," Cassandra shouted, then skipped to the doorway.

"You really must do something about the child before you begin working here." Miss Adelaide shook her head and laughed. "She seems full of vinegar."

"Today, at least. I'm enjoying the child I discovered on the walk very much."

"Good. Just remember to keep a firm hand with her from these early moments. You set the tone of your relationship."

There might be truth to the words, but they seemed harsh. "The child's just arrived from a war zone. I'm sure we'll be fine."

Miss Adelaide shook her head and looked toward the ceiling. "I'll pray you are."

Cassandra stuck her head back in the door. "Can we go find a park now?"

Josie nodded. "Just a moment. I'll see if Miss Adelaide has some ideas for us."

Miss Adelaide quickly checked out Cassandra's books and one for Josie. "There's the beautiful Eden Park on the other side of your home. I'd start there. See you next week."

Josie gathered the child and headed toward home. "We'll try the park on a day that we have a picnic packed. How's that?"

"All right." Disappointment colored Cassandra's words, and

Josie determined to get her to a park as soon as possible.

She held tightly to Cassandra's hand as the child skipped next to her. The skipping seemed to loosen her tongue, and the child talked the whole way home. That ease disappeared as soon as Josie started lunch preparations. She stared in the icebox looking for inspiration.

"Do you have anything good today?"

"How about a sandwich? Maybe some chips and fruit?"

"Any fish to go with the chips, ma'am?"

Josie chewed on her lower lip. She didn't care for fish, so never bought it. If it would make Cassandra content, she would run downstairs to see if the grocer had any. No, that was crazy. Better keep things simple. "Not today. Ham sandwiches are the menu. We'll get fish the next time we shop. You'll have to let me know other foods you enjoy, so I can keep them in stock."

Cassandra's nose scrunched. "Can we go today?"

Josie laughed. "No, sweetie. We have to eat what we have first. Waste not, want not."

"Then I suppose ham will do."

"Why don't you go read a book while I get the plates ready?"

The afternoon passed quietly as Cassandra read her books and Josie cleaned. A burble of delight filled Josie. Maybe this experience wouldn't be as easy as she imagined. But Cassandra was filling a space in their small family.

twelve

"Cassandra, time for breakfast."

Silence answered the words. Josie tiptoed down the hall to Cassandra's small room. Cassandra lay on her side, curled around her doll, tears streaming down her cheeks. Josie watched a moment, unsure what to do but knowing she wanted to comfort the poor child. She eased into the room and knelt beside the bed. She stroked the child's tangled curls. "Sweetie. I'm so sorry."

Cassandra's silent tears turned to sobs that wracked her small frame. "I want my mum."

"I know, darling. I so wish you could be with her." Josie struggled for words as tears threatened to overflow her eyes. "You must miss her."

"Awfully." The word shuddered from Cassandra. She scrubbed her face and tried to sit up. "Sorry, ma'am. I'll stop crying." Tears continued to stream, and Josie reached out to swipe one away but stilled when the child flinched.

Josie cleared her throat. "Should we write her a letter today? Let her know how you are?"

The little girl nodded. "I'd like that."

"Let's get you some breakfast. Then we'll get out some paper and pencils. I know she'd love to get mail from you."

"But the post won't deliver it for ever so long."

"Maybe. But we can keep sending letters, knowing she'll read them eventually. And with each letter, she'll be so happy to know what you're doing and that you're safe."

Cassandra frowned. "I haven't done much."

"Then we'll change that."

The conversation played through Josie's mind during breakfast, chores, and the balance of the day. She and Art needed to do something to give the child plenty to fill letters. Even simple outings would fit the bill. When Art arrived home and Cassandra was settled for the night, Josie sat on the couch next to him, ready to plan their attack.

"We really need to do something to occupy her mind. The child is focused almost exclusively on what's happening at home."

"That's natural, I'd imagine."

"Probably true, but it will be easier for her if we can give her things to anticipate."

"Okay." Art pulled at his pockets playfully. "Remember, we aren't made of money."

"I know, but maybe your family would help, especially since Cassandra is part of the family."

"I'd rather not ask."

Josie snuggled closer to his side. "Okay. I'll keep the outings inexpensive."

"What did you have in mind?"

"Things like the Sunlite Pool, movies, ice cream. It doesn't have to be extravagant. The library every day won't satisfy her. She told me she hadn't done anything that she could tell her mom about."

Art laughed as he wrapped an arm around Josie. "Not everyone takes pleasure in libraries like you, darling."

"Definitely their loss."

"Maybe. These other options sound good as long as we spread them out with things like picnics or outings to the parks."

"Then we'll start this weekend. A movie and some ice cream. Maybe we can even find *Pinocchio* playing somewhere." Josie tipped her head and kissed his cheek. He turned and claimed her lips. Josie relaxed into his kiss.

≈

Saturday morning Art woke slowly. It felt good to relax without the pressures of work weighing on him. Mr. Fine continued to put pressure on the white-collar employees to see into the future. If Art could do that, he wouldn't be working for a small company like this. He rubbed hands across his face, trying to brush the vestiges of sleep away.

Josie didn't lie next to him. He'd hoped to hold her for a moment, but she'd bounded out of bed before he could. He turned on his side and considered getting up. A soft sound reached his ears. It was muffled, but clear.

Was this what Josie had dealt with most of the week?

He cringed at the thought of comforting a crying child. What did he know about girls? He waited, hoping Josie would take care of Cassandra, but her footsteps didn't pad toward the door. He gulped and pushed out of the bed. After grabbing his robe, he faltered outside her room. Wails replaced the quiet cries.

Surely she would stop. Without his intervention. She had to. Right?

Tears baffled him.

And there'd been so many in this apartment. He barely knew what to do with Josie's. What on earth was he supposed to do with a little girl he barely knew? Promise her a pony? Give her his car? He considered doing both, then slapped himself on the forehead.

"You're a well-educated man. You can handle an eight-year-old." The pep talk did little to get him out of the doorway.

Cassandra looked up, her face blotchy from the crying.

"Can I get you anything?" The words sounded inane even as they slipped by him. He cleared his throat. "How about I get you a drink of water?"

Her face crumpled. She whimpered, and he looked around her room, desperate for something that would comfort. There. Her doll had fallen under the bed. He knelt before her and picked up the doll. "Were you missing her?"

Cassandra frowned but swallowed hard against her tears. "No, sir. Missing me brother and da."

"Tell me why."

"On Saturdays, we'd always do something together. Hike

across a park. Splash in a pool. Play rugby or football."

Art straightened. This he could do. "Josie and I have planned some outings for you, too. How would you like to go to an amusement park today?"

"Sir?"

"You know. A place with rides and roller coasters."

"I don't know about that." She shrunk back into herself.

Art backpedaled. "How about we go to the pool there and you can watch the rides. See if it's something you'd like to try in the future. Think that might work?"

She nodded. "I'd like to try."

"All right. Let's get up then. Josie probably has a good breakfast ready. Then we can prepare for our adventure."

The morning passed quickly as Josie prepared a picnic for them, and they climbed into the Packard. Cassandra remained quiet but took an interest in their surroundings as they drove.

He glanced at her through the rearview mirror. "How's Cincinnati compare to England?"

"It's not as crowded. The folks seem stand-offish."

Josie turned around to look over the seat. "Stand-offish? Who?"

"That Miss Adelaide hasn't warmed to me yet."

"It's your charming personality, Cassie. All that rushing about at the library keeps her on edge."

The banter continued until he reached the park. After paying the entry fee, they ventured into the area around the pool. It was supposed to be one of the largest pools in the country, and looking at its size of two hundred by four hundred feet, Art believed it. If Cassandra wandered off, they might lose her amid the crowd.

"Stay with one of us. No wandering."

Cassandra rolled her eyes as only an exasperated eight-year-old can. "Yes, sir."

"I'm serious, Cassandra. I've heard it holds ten thousand people. I'd hate to lose you so soon after you arrive."

"I'm not an infant." Indignation filled her voice.

"I know. But stay close."

"We're fine, Art. There aren't nearly that many people here." Josie grabbed Cassandra's hand. "Let's explore a bit. Find the best spot to settle down."

Art followed as the girls picked their way through the crowd. He gladly dropped the towels and toys when the gals chose a spot. From here, he could see a wide stretch of the pool. Enough to give Cassandra some freedom.

Cassandra pulled off her blouse and skirt and rushed in her swimsuit into the water.

"I hope she can swim." Josie's voice held a tinge of concern. "Why don't you go with her? Make sure she's okay."

Art nodded. Probably a good idea while they determined her skill level. In no time, Cassandra had talked him into the deeper areas of the pool, and he was roughhousing with her. The girl's giggles reverberated across the water. He could get used to days like this.

❧

The days slid from the calendar, Josie trying to keep up with Cassandra and Art. Those two had settled into an easy relationship since their time at the pool. She was almost as active as Kat, and Josie looked for ways to get her involved in sports or other activities. Josie toyed with the idea of signing up Cassandra for a basketball team at the YWCA. What would Cassandra's mother think if her daughter went home a tomboy? Probably not much, since Cassandra had indicated she played sports like rugby and football. Or was this a way of protesting her placement? Josie was at a loss to know, so did the only thing she could.

"Cassie, how'd you like to join a basketball team?"

Cassandra looked up from the book in her lap. "Basketball?"

"It's an American sport. You run up and down a court and throw a ball into baskets on the wall. My sister likes to play it, and there's a place near here with teams."

"I don't know."

"Kat enjoys it, but she plays baseball, too."

"I'll give it a go."

Josie took Cassandra to the YWCA. After her first practice, the drive passed in silence. When they'd about reached the house, Josie cleared her throat. "What did you think?"

"There's an awful lot of running and throwing the ball."

Josie laughed. "That's right. It's integral to the game."

"I'm not sure if it's for me, but I'll try again if you like."

"I think I do. In fact, I think I'll take a fitness class at the same time."

They'd barely reached the house when Annabelle stopped by. Cassandra had hopped in the bathtub, so Josie led Annabelle to the living room. Once Annabelle had settled on the couch with a Coke, she grilled Josie on how the transition had gone.

"Is Cassandra settled?"

"I think she's adjusting. We're doing all we can to help her." Josie chewed on the jagged edge of a fingernail.

"How?"

"The child never stops moving, so I'm looking for activities for her. We're trying a basketball team at the YWCA. We walk to the library and places like that. Anything I can think of to get us out of the apartment often. I knew the apartment was small but had no idea how one added body, especially one so small, would make it seem tiny."

"The activity is good for her. Should keep her healthy and her mind occupied."

"It does seem to help. While she loved the trip to the Sunlite Pool, we can't afford to do that as often as she'd like."

"Let's find some alternatives then."

The two shared ideas for a bit, and Josie took satisfaction in the fact that Annabelle's list didn't contain anything she hadn't already considered.

"Maybe take walks to Eden Park as a family."

"I don't know that Art will want to walk back through there each night."

"You could meet him on his way home."

"That's a great idea." Josie sipped her Coke. "From her reading and letter writing, I can tell she'll do fine in school." • She clasped her hands around the glass and sighed. "She's starting to relax, but still tends toward formality. Thanking us for every little thing we do."

Annabelle considered her words. "Any flashes of frustration or tears? I'm seeing a lot of that with the children. It's as if they've been trained to be very polite. But the strain eventually burdens them. Their emotions bounce all over."

"There are tears, but not any more than you'd expect for a child who's been separated from her family. Is there anything we can do to help her?"

"Give her time and love. She'll calm."

Josie considered the words after Annabelle left. She just needed to stay the course. But it felt like she should do something more to ease Cassandra's transition. Especially considering there was no planned end date. It could be a long war if Cassandra couldn't settle into their home. If only other evacuated children lived near. She made a note to ask Annabelle the next time they talked.

Regardless of those concerns, she had to get Cassandra registered for school. In fact, the pattern of school coupled with the chance to meet American kids might help immensely. After a morning at the library, Josie and Cassandra walked to the neighborhood school. While Cassandra had attended a private school at home, there was no way Art and Josie could afford to send her to one. No, she would experience the fullness of American life by attending the public school. Cassandra trudged after her, a frown tipping the corners of her mouth down.

"Must I go to school?"

Josie laughed. "Yes, miss. I know your folks would think your education is critical. Parents are funny that way."

"I don't know they'll like me learning American history."

"Sorry but that's your option here. Guess you'll be ahead of your classmates in that area when you go home."

Cassandra tucked her small, gloved hand in Josie's. "Thank you for all the effort for me."

"Happy to. You're good practice for the day I have children of my own." Pain squeezed through her, but she shoved it to the side. "Besides, it will be good for you to meet some children. Make some friends while you're here."

"But I won't be here long enough."

"I hope that's true. Even if it is, think of it as developing pen pals."

Cassandra's grimace made it clear she wasn't buying that argument. "Maybe."

"Stiff upper lip and all that." Cassandra's surprised look rewarded Josie. "I'm learning a thing or two by listening to you."

"Right."

Josie squeezed Cassandra's hand. "Now let's get you squared away. You'll love it."

thirteen

"Wilson, I need to see you. Now." E. K. Fine's voice bellowed through the room. The others turned to watch his reaction.

"Coming, sir."

Tension stretched across his neck and shoulders. Could anything good come from being called into the boss's office? Art sucked in a deep breath and let it out slowly.

Art barely reached the glass-front office before Mr. Fine started talking. He paced back and forth behind his desk as he talked, using a cigar to punctuate the air.

"Wilson, you've done a fine job with the books. You've marshaled the numbers effectively. Even I can understand them." He chuckled while Art watched, unsure how to respond. "Just a little humor. Anyway, I called you in here for a new project."

Art stood taller. That sounded like good news.

"I'm sending you to Chicago for a series of meetings. There are some manufacturers there who are further down the road for switching to a war economy. I want you to meet with them, see what they did, and determine if any of that can work here. The key to success is to always be a step ahead of all the other companies. There will be a limited number of contracts, and I want us to land at least one. We can't be unprepared."

"Yes, sir. Any particular industry?"

"Use common sense. You'll be fine."

"Anything we can learn from what the company did during the last war?"

"No. Even if there was, that ended twenty years ago. Not relevant to today."

Art nodded. Guess the man didn't live by the maxim that those who can't remember the past are condemned to repeat it.

"When do I leave?"

"Tomorrow. My secretary has your train ticket."

"How long?"

"Plan on a week."

Art grimaced. Josie would not be thrilled to have him leaving. Especially on such short notice.

"Art? Any problems?" The look on Fine's face communicated the answer should be no.

He'd promised to take Josie to a show tomorrow night. Doris had agreed to watch Cassandra so the two of them could get some time alone. She would be disappointed if that didn't work out. After a steeling breath, Art said, "I can't leave tomorrow, sir."

"And why not? You should be pleased with the opportunity."

"I am, but I have plans with my wife."

"That?" E.K. waved his hand as if swatting a fly. "That's not a problem. Leave now, pack, take her out tonight instead. The missus will understand."

While a good theory, in practice Art doubted it would hold up. They weren't newlyweds without responsibilities now. Doris might not have the freedom to adjust her schedule and watch Cassandra.

E.K. sat back in his chair, fingers steepled in front of his face.

"I'll get that ticket now."

"Good man. Don't let me down."

Art strode from the room then halted at the secretary's desk. She handed him the ticket with an apologetic smile. "The others will meet you at Union Terminal at seven."

"Yes, ma'am."

"That's a.m."

"I understand." Art grabbed the ticket and returned to his desk. What would he need for these meetings? E.K. couldn't have been more vague if he'd tried. He sank into his chair unsure what to do.

Stan came and stood in front of Art's desk. Leaning against

it, he smirked. "Ready for our trip?"

"Are we the only ones going?"

"Nope. Choirboy's coming, too."

While Stan meant that as a pejorative term, some of Art's tension eased at the realization Charlie would join them. Art wouldn't have to deal with Stan alone, and Charlie had the experience with the company to have a good grasp on what it could do if it switched focus. Better yet, it meant reinforcements when standing up to Stan.

"It'll be good to have him along."

Charlie grinned from his desk. "We'll team up on Stan."

"Sure. You think that. I'll keep you hopping."

"As long as it's not from bar to bar."

Art laughed at Charlie's earnest expression. Charlie winked at him. Yeah, this trip would be okay. Josie would be okay. Josie. He was supposed to head home. "I'll let you two handle packing what we'll need for the trip. I'm under orders to go home and see my wife."

"See, that's why I'll never marry." Stan snickered. "Why be tied down to a dame who wants to keep you home and in her lair all the time."

"There are benefits."

"Nothing I can't get already."

Charlie shook his head in disgust. "You are hopeless, Stan."

"Maybe, but at least I'm not tied down."

Art changed his mind. Maybe it would still be a long week with Stan.

❧

"You have to do what?" Josie couldn't believe Art was leaving. Travel wasn't part of his job. What about their night out? She'd looked forward to it all week. And how could he help with Cassandra if he wasn't here? School started soon, which would bring a new set of adjustments to Cassandra's life.

"We can go out tonight, and then I'll pack."

He said it so matter-of-factly, as if plans could change in an instant.

"But we can't leave Cassandra alone. Who can stay with her on such short notice?" She dug her fingernails into her palms to distract herself from the building tears.

Art sighed and pulled her into his lap. "I don't like it either, but the boss made it clear I have to go. If it's important to the company, then it has to be important to us, too. It's only for a week, after all."

"You're right." His arms slipped around her, and she leaned into him. "I can still hate the idea."

"I know."

Josie tried to push up, but he held on. "Let me see if Doris can come tonight."

"She can." His voice had turned husky. "Come here."

She stilled as he reached up to kiss her. She sank into his embrace as the kiss deepened. Art ran his fingers through her hair, and her thoughts muddled.

"Miss Josie?"

Josie startled and pushed away from Art. Patting her hair, she turned to see Cassandra standing in the doorway. "Yes?"

Cassandra's brow furrowed. "Did you say you're leaving tonight?"

"Just for a bit." Josie licked her lips, considering how to ease Cassandra's fears. "Doris from downstairs will come up and stay with you."

"I don't need someone."

"You'll have fun. You know how much you enjoy Mrs. Duncan. She'll probably have you help her with cookies."

Cassandra crossed her arms, chin jutted.

"Come here, sweetie." Cassandra reluctantly walked across the room and joined them. Josie smoothed her curls. "It'll be fine. We'll be back about bedtime."

Cassandra eased next to her. "Promise?"

"Yes." Josie's heart ached at the fear in that one word. She hugged Cassandra. "Now let me get ready. And make plans for tomorrow night. It'll be just us girls, and one of the last nights before school starts."

A wistful smile touched the girl's face. "I'd like that."

Art watched her go. "I hate to leave as school starts."

"Don't worry. We'll suffer through." Josie poked him in the ribs. "Let's get out of here."

&

Art slipped out the next morning with a light kiss on Josie's forehead. The feathery touch teased her out of sleep in time to watch him leave, and then roll back over. She relaxed into the mattress, the things she needed to do flashing through her mind. Work at the library in the morning and then take Cassandra shopping for some school items. The child's small suitcase hadn't contained nearly enough options. Two outfits, underwear, and pajamas didn't qualify. Josie's part-time pay would help purchase the extra items the child needed, and a small sum had arrived from England to help with the costs.

After a quick breakfast of toast and tea, they headed to the library. Josie saw Cassandra ensconced in a quiet corner before settling herself in at the circulation desk. Cassandra must have found a set of books that delighted her, because she stayed in place for the morning. Josie wandered over to her side.

"What did you find to read?"

Cassandra tugged her gaze from the pages to Josie's face. "*Little House on the Prairie.* Was it really like this?"

"I don't know. Despite what you may think, I didn't actually live then." Josie tousled Cassie's curls. "But I like the way she describes life back then."

Cassandra closed the book and held it to her chest. "May I check it out?"

"Absolutely."

"Okay. May I please go outside for a bit?"

Josie considered Cassandra. "For a bit. But no getting dirty. We have to get your school things after this."

Cassandra placed the book on the circulation desk, then skipped out of the building. Josie stayed busy helping folks find books. Right as she'd begun to wonder what Cassandra was up to, the child came in with a couple of daises.

"These are for you."

"Thank you, Cassandra." The child beamed from the praise. "They look a tad thirsty. Let me find a vase or glass to put them in." Josie found a cup shoved in the back reaches of the desk. "Here. Why don't you fill it with water and wash your hands. Then I think we'll leave."

Cassandra skipped toward the washroom. The sunshine had warmed her cheeks, and the wind had mussed her hair.

After returning home long enough to leave the flowers on the counter, the two drove downtown. Soon she found a parking space near several of the stores she planned to visit. Josie enjoyed browsing, but Cassandra acted overwhelmed by the selections. As they strolled the racks, Josie pulled out option after option.

"Would you like the playsuit or the skirt only?" The red plaid was cheery and played well with Cassandra's complexion.

"I'd rather not have either, please."

"Why not?"

"I don't think my mother would like me to have either one."

Josie stared at the child. "I don't understand why not. You must have clothes for school. And either of these options should work."

"Well, I don't like them." Cassandra turned away from Josie.

"I can't send you to school in one of two outfits. After all, the one at home needs some serious mending, and I can't wash clothes every night."

Cassandra shifted from side to side. "Mum didn't send money with me. I can't pay."

"Sweetie, she wired some for things like this. If it's not enough, it's all right. Art and I are happy to take care of them. Now which one do you like?"

Slowly Cassandra caught the spirit of school shopping and jumped in. Before long, she wanted one of everything and Josie had to rein her in.

Once the shopping was over, Josie smiled at the surprise she'd planned. They stowed the bags in the backseat of the Packard and headed out to the zoo. Cassandra's eyes got round when she realized where they were.

"The zoo? Are we really going in?"

Josie laughed. "Of course we are. One last hurrah before school begins. Besides, someone's waiting for us." Josie parked the car and glanced at her watch. Hopefully, they'd arrived in time to catch one of Susie the gorilla's shows. Miss Adelaide had told her it was quite a sight to watch the gorilla cavort with her trainer. Josie hoped it brought joy to Cassandra.

Josie grabbed Cassandra's hand and walked through the park toward the show. While the gorilla entertained the crowd, Josie delighted in watching Cassandra's reaction. The girl beamed as they strolled through the zoo afterwards. And the smile didn't fade as she prepared for bed.

Josie tucked Cassandra in and prayed with her. Several new outfits lined the dresser in Cassandra's room. Cassandra had sparkled as she organized them and lined them up in her room. Now Josie's prayers shifted to finding a friend for Cassandra, someone who could ease her little-girl loneliness.

She walked through the apartment, straightening as she went. Now that Cassandra was in bed, the place felt too quiet. Josie missed Art. His presence made the apartment home. Without him, everything felt a bit off.

There was so much she wanted to share with him—the little details of the day she enjoyed sharing when he came home each night. But for now she would wait.

fourteen

The day's meetings had finally ended. Art couldn't decide if this trip constituted a fool's errand. He sat all day with nothing to contribute as folks debated how they could evolve their companies to meet the demands of a war economy. As far as he could tell, there was no indication the United States would actually enter the war. Let China and Japan duke it out in the Far East while Germany and Italy fought the rest of Europe.

"Come on, guys. Time to head out." Stan waggled his eyebrows. "Enjoy the sights of Chicago."

Art stifled a sigh. Each night the same thing: Stan badgering Charlie and him to go anywhere but the hotel. "Your idea of the sights differs from mine."

"You are such dead weight."

Charlie laughed and bumped Stan. "I don't think that's what you mean. You know you're welcome to join us."

"Not my idea of a good time." Stan stalked off.

Art watched him go. Yet again he thanked God for Charlie's presence. "What kind of shape do you think he'll be in tomorrow?"

"The good Lord's the only one who knows." He clapped Art on the shoulder. "Let's grab a bite."

They walked several blocks until they found a tiny Chinese restaurant. The aroma of ginger, garlic, and other things Art couldn't name collided in a way that made his stomach rumble.

"So your thoughts?"

Art looked up from his egg drop soup and blinked. "On what?"

"How we're supposed to keep the company afloat."

"You think E.K. really cares what we think?"

Charlie shook his head. "Doesn't matter. What matters is that if we want to continue to have jobs, we must think creatively."

"I think we're wasting our time. We're not in a war."

"I pray you're right. However, our allies have to get their munitions and other supplies from somewhere. It might as well be us."

"Have you forgotten we make pianos? Do you expect them to start dropping grand pianos as bombs?"

Charlie's rich chuckle filled the air. "That's a creative idea. Might be too expensive and unwieldy. . ."

"You're nuts."

"Just going with your idea." Charlie paused as the waitress brought steaming bowls of rice topped with different sauces and meats to the table. "But it's time to get serious. Come up with a proactive plan. So when the day—"

"If the day. . ." Art jumped in.

Charlie nodded. "Okay. If the day comes, we're ready to help the company that pays our bills compete."

When he put it that way, Art had to agree. "What about plane parts?"

"Maybe." Charlie's wrinkled brow indicated his skepticism. "That's the kind of thinking I'm after. What kind of parts do you mean?"

They spent the balance of the meal trying to come up with ways to use the processes and materials they already had. Hopefully, they'd be ready.

❧

Four days later, Art opened the front door and tossed his suitcase on the floor. "Josie. I'm back."

Those words had never sounded so good to his ears. The week away from home had been long. While he hoped it benefited E. K. Fine Pianos, he belonged right here with his girls.

Josie squealed and ran out of the kitchen. In two steps, Art picked her up and spun her around the living room.

"I have missed you so much, gorgeous." He set her down and gazed into her eyes. "I didn't think you could become more beautiful, but you did."

Josie leaned her cheek against his cheek. "I've missed you, too."

He held her a moment, savoring the feeling. The seven days had felt like seventy. But the moment he walked through the door, he'd known. He was home. His kissed her with an intensity that had her leaning into him. Slowly, he pulled back until his gaze locked with hers. A soft smile played across her face. He ran his thumb along her cheek, and then turned. "Where's my other girl?"

Josie frowned. "She's downstairs with Doris. We needed a bit of space from each other."

"Things going that well?"

"She's struggling with school."

"In the first week? Is it academics?"

"Nooo." Josie chuckled. "The child has already been bumped up a grade, and it may happen again. No, she's a British child thrust into an American school."

Art scratched his head. Josie meant for him to pick up on something, but he wasn't getting it. Nope. Wasn't coming to him. He shrugged. "You'll have to help me."

"She won't say the pledge."

"The Pledge of Allegiance?"

"That's the one. She says she's not an American, so she won't pledge to a flag that isn't hers." Josie looked over his shoulder at the door. "I don't know that I blame her, but. . ."

"It does put us in a spot."

"I'm not worried about us. I'd hoped she'd make friends at school, but this isn't helping her cause. At all."

Ah, so that was the issue. "Has she mentioned wanting friends?"

"No, and that's the problem. She puts up this front that she doesn't need any. But you should see her watch the other kids."

Art tugged Josie away from the door. "Keep your voice down. What if she hears?"

"I honestly don't think she'd care." Josie straightened his tie, played with his collar. "Cassandra's a turtle pulling into her shell. She's done so well with us, but this is somehow different."

"She's probably homesick. Misses her school and friends there."

"I know. But she could be here a long time. She's not working to make the best of that."

"Could that be her age? She's only eight."

Josie's sigh lingered as if pushed up from her toes. "These first weeks are critical. If she wants to make friends, she needs to pick her battles carefully. Refusing to say the pledge isn't the best foot to start on."

The door squeaked on its hinges as it swung open. Art turned, a broad smile on his face when he saw Cassandra. He stepped toward her and hunched to her level. "How's my girl?"

Cassandra's face crumpled then hardened. "I'm not your girl."

She raced past him to her room and slammed the door.

"Welcome to my world." Josie grimaced. "We have to find a way to reach her, Art. I can't stand the thought that the rest of her time here is going to be miserable."

Art agreed. The only problem was he had no idea what to suggest or do. Maybe he should go back to Chicago.

❧

Josie struggled to fight the fog of sleep. The quilt kept her pressed to the bed, even as her brain argued that somebody needed her. A soft mewling pulled at her. She shook her head, trying to clear it. Cassandra? She shook off the blanket, and Art snuffled in his sleep. Faint moonlight lit her steps as she padded to the door.

Through the crack, she heard the soft cries. Poor child.

Heart heavy, Josie eased into Cassandra's room. The girl

tossed on the bed, caught in the throes of another nightmare. "Please, Mummy. Please."

Josie perched on the edge of the bed. *Father, surround this child with Your arms. Bring peace to every fiber of her being. Only You can calm her and give her the assurance that she will never be alone and that she is safe.* She leaned down and pulled Cassandra into her arms. The child stirred, then slowly opened her eyes. The tension in her body eased when she recognized Josie.

"I'm not in London?"

"No, you're safe here in Cincinnati."

"What about my mum?"

"I don't know, sweetie. But I'll stay with you for a while. Go back to sleep."

Josie prayed until a soft dawn eased across the early morning sky and Cassandra slipped back to sleep. As she stroked Cassandra's golden curls, tears fell down Josie's cheeks—tears for the child before her and the torment she felt. But also for the child she didn't have. The one that she hadn't even known if it was a boy or girl. While God knew and held that child, Josie wished she'd had a chance—even once—to see her baby.

Instead, she'd pray for Cassandra, the child entrusted to her. That she could do.

By the time Art got up and was ready for the day, Josie had slipped into a simple, flour-bag dress and prepared coffee and eggs. He gobbled the food while skimming the newspaper. As she sipped some coffee heavily flavored with cream and sugar, she watched him. Her nose wrinkled as he drank his coffee black. Ugh.

Headlines highlighted the continued intensity of the air raids over Britain. Bombers had dropped their payloads over London. Josie would have to remind Art to take the paper to work so Cassandra couldn't see the headline. Such news could only turn her dreams to more nightmares.

"Any plans for today?" Art's words made the paper vibrate.

"Hmm? Get Cassandra to school. Pray she makes some

friends and begins to settle in to the routine. Spend a few hours at the library. Then join Doris for a new Bible study."

"Sounds like a full day."

"I suppose." Now that she thought about it, life was busier, fuller since Cassandra had arrived. Whatever the reason, it pleased her. "I doubt I'll work at the library much longer."

Art looked up from the paper. "Why not?"

"Miss Adelaide has been back for a week now."

"You'll miss the work." It wasn't a question, but a statement that showed how well Art understood her.

Josie shrugged, trying to hide how much it did matter. "If it comes to that, yes. I guess I'll have time to volunteer somewhere else. I've gotten used to having somewhere to go."

"Maybe you'll get pregnant again, and we'll have a baby to keep you occupied." He said the words so casually, while they ripped at the scab on her heart. A stab of fear punctured her at the thought of another pregnancy ending like the first.

She didn't feel recovered from this miscarriage. But clearly, Art had placed it completely behind him. How could he do that? Her nose started to tingle, and she bit on her tongue to distract herself. She wouldn't waste the tears on someone who didn't understand the depths of her pain. Besides, God was piecing her heart back together. Cassandra seemed to fill part of that process.

Art glanced at his watch. "We've got a couple minutes for our Bible reading."

Josie eased onto the chair next to him. She needed this time to connect and find peace before the day erupted around her. As Art read Psalm 91, Josie listened to the words, letting them flow over her.

Art finished, then pushed back from the table. "See you tonight." He paused, connecting with her gaze. "I know God has something for you."

As he rushed out the door, Josie fought the surge of frustration. His words sounded trite, an afterthought meant to placate her. That wasn't what she needed. She didn't know what she needed. A manual for how to reach a shell-shocked and bitter child? Instructions on how to create a community in a new city that still felt foreign after ten months?

What she did know? Time to get Cassandra up and walk her to school. And hope the teacher didn't have any other surprise news like the pledge fiasco.

fifteen

"Josie." Doris huffed up the stairs, her words trembling ahead of her.

Josie stuck her head out the door. "Yes, ma'am."

"Thank goodness you're home." Doris stopped and sucked in a breath. "You've got a call downstairs. Said she was your sister."

Why would Kat call her? Josie looked from Doris to the door. "Can I get you anything?"

"Go on ahead. I'll just catch my breath."

"Yes, ma'am." Josie brushed past Doris and hurried to the back room of the grocery store. Someday it would be so nice to have a phone in the apartment for privacy. At least they didn't get many calls. She picked up the receiver. "This is Josie."

The wire crackled and popped. She pulled it tighter to her ear. "Hello?"

"That you?"

Josie could barely make out the words. "Yes."

"This is Kat. We made it to a championship this weekend. You'll come, won't you?"

"Who made it to what?"

The sigh was strong enough Josie could imagine Kat rolling her eyes. "My baseball team, silly. We made it to the big tournament. You have to come."

"I'll check with Art. I don't think we have anything going on."

Kat squealed. "Then you'll come."

Josie laughed. To have the enthusiasm of an "in-between-er." "I'll see what we can do. When do we need to be there?"

Kat filled her in on all the details. "And be sure to bring Cassandra with you. We all want to meet her. Does she have the best accent in the world? Can you understand what she says? What does she think about Cincinnati?"

111

"You can ask her those questions when you meet her."

"Make sure you're here Friday night, so we can get an early start Saturday. You won't want to miss a game. Bye." Like that, Kat was off and on to her next event.

Josie shook her head. Mr. Duncan stuck his head around the corner.

"Everything okay?"

"Yes, sir. Thanks for getting me."

"No problem. Doris enjoys an excuse to hustle up them stairs."

His wry look left her chuckling as she hiked up those same stairs. When she entered the apartment, Doris sat on the sofa, flipping through Josie's Bible. A stab of something, violation maybe, flashed through Josie.

"Find what you're looking for?"

"No. I'm looking for an elusive verse. Ah well. It'll come to me. Probably in the middle of the night, but they always come."

Josie perched on the wing chair. If they spent the weekend in Dayton, she needed to pack. Figure out what they would need at the ball diamonds.

"Well, I'll head back down. Tell Cassandra I'll have fresh cookies for her."

"She'll probably smell them and stop before she comes here."

Doris shut the door behind her. Time to pack.

❧

Art hurried up the stairs. The next place they lived would be closer to the ground. Today he didn't have the energy to charge the steps like usual. He opened the door to a whirlwind of activity. Josie had two bags lying next to the couch.

"Going somewhere?"

Josie looked up at him with a coquettish smile. "How's a weekend in Dayton sound?"

"Honestly? Terrible." All he wanted was a quiet weekend. Maybe take Cassandra for some ice cream. Keep life simple. Yeah, that sounded really good. Until he looked at Josie's face. "I take it we're going."

"Kat's team is in a tournament, and she wants us there."

While there were many things Art didn't know about Josie, it had been clear from the beginning her family took priority. That made them his priority, too. Guess they'd make the trek. "When do we need to arrive?"

"Not sure when the games start tomorrow. Could we drive tonight?"

"Is that why the bags are packed?"

She had the grace to wear a sheepish look. "Do you mind?"

"As long as you're happy, it's fine with me."

The door opened behind him. He turned to see Cassandra, cookie crumbs dotting her chin. "Doris sent extra sugar cookies up with me." She stared at the bags, a frown growing on her face. "What's all this?"

"How'd you like to go on a weekend adventure?" Josie's voice begged her to share the excitement. "We'll stay with my family and watch Kat play baseball games."

Cassandra wrinkled her nose. "You promised to take me to the movies."

"We will." Josie looked at Art before continuing. "In fact, I bet we'll go while we're in Dayton. We can't watch baseball all day. Besides, this is another American sport. You've enjoyed basketball, and I think you'll like this, too. Better yet, you'll get to meet my family."

❧

Art picked up the first couple bags. "Will we eat here first?"

"I've got supper ready."

"All right. I'll load the bags, then we can eat and get out the door." The tournament could be competitive since Kat played on a good team. And Mark might have time to play some games this trip. Josie's Mom would dote on Cassandra. Everybody needed extra mothering from time to time. Especially girls thousands of miles from home.

An hour later, he'd loaded the Packard and they'd eaten. The wheels turned as they made their way to Dayton. Art cracked his window and let the breeze blow through the vehicle. When they pulled in front of the Millers' home around nine o'clock, welcoming lights blazed in each window.

Art parked at the curb. "Do they know we're coming?"

"I'm sure Kat told them." Josie shrugged like it didn't matter one way or another. She was probably right.

The front door bounced open and a flash of checked fabric raced to the car. When it stopped, he saw it was Kat.

❧

"You made it!" Kat's words ran on top of each other, bringing a smile to Josie's face.

"I promised we would."

"No, you said you'd talk to Art. That doesn't mean much until you're here." Kat smiled so big her face almost cracked. "You got here in time to watch my team win the whole contest."

Art laughed. "Nice to see your ego's still intact." He urged Cassandra forward. "I'd like you to meet Cassandra Wilson. Cassandra, this is my sister-in-law, Katherine Miller."

Kat stuck out her hand. "Pleased to meet you, Cassandra. But you can call me Kat. Katherine is way too long of a name to yell across a baseball diamond."

"What are we going to do with you?" Josie pretended to frown but had a feeling Kat saw right through her. Somehow Kat knew the world would revolve around her whims. If that meant playing baseball with the boys, so be it. She'd never let anything slow her down—and she'd just turned fourteen.

Cassandra grabbed Josie's arm and hung on.

"Don't worry, Cassandra. You and I will become friends. Maybe even grab an ice-cream cone after the games."

"Could we get a sweet, too?"

"I don't see why not."

Cassandra's face lit up.

"Let's introduce you to Mom and Dad." Kat led a willing Cassandra into the house.

Art slipped an arm around Josie's waist. "Do you think we could have her move in with us?"

"Who?"

"Kat, of course. Other than you, I haven't seen anyone else get Cassandra to trust them that quickly."

Josie leaned her head against Art's arm as they strolled up the walk. "Call it the Miller girl charm." She felt the rumble of his laugh, and it pleased her. "Though you do well with her, too. She lights up when you're home spending time with her. Ready to cheer Kat on?"

"We wouldn't be here if I wasn't." He patted his jacket pocket. "I've got a magazine or two stashed for the dull periods."

Josie pulled away from him and playfully slapped him. "There will be no dull moments."

"Of course not." Art held his hands in front of him. "It's the Boy Scout in me. I like to be prepared for anything."

"On your best behavior, Art. You don't want Kat to hear."

"No, ma'am. Can't guarantee good behavior." His face took on a long pious look.

"Why on earth not?"

"You have to buy my good behavior."

"I don't do it with Cassandra, so why on earth would I do that with a big guy like you?" Josie crossed her arms and stared at him.

"Because it's a small fee really. Just a kiss."

"A kiss?" Josie made a show of tapping her finger on her mouth and thinking about his proposal. She hoped he wouldn't notice the warmth spreading across her cheeks. "All right, but you'd better kiss me good and long."

A slow, Cheshire cat grin spread across Art's face, until his dimple appeared on his left cheek. "My pleasure."

❧

Once everyone had met Cassandra, Mother showed them to their rooms. Cassandra would bunk with Kat, and Josie and Art had her small room. They slipped into bed so they'd be ready for the morning. Cassandra jumped into their bed as soon as the sun's rays filled the room with light.

"Is it time to leave yet?"

Josie peeked at the child. Cassandra fairly vibrated from

where she'd bounced. "I can't wait to watch Kat play."

"What time is it?"

"Seven."

"Let Kat get you breakfast, and we'll be down in a bit."

Cassandra bounced out of the room, then Josie rolled over with a groan.

"What was that?" Art's muffled words drifted out from under the pillow he'd pulled over his head.

"That would be your cousin. We might as well get up and ready for the day."

An hour later, Josie's family joined them for the game. As Mark bantered with their dad, Art settled back, providing Josie a place to lean. Rain the night before had knocked down the dust, and the crowd yelled encouragement and jeers, depending on their loyalties.

After they'd been at the ball fields a couple hours, Josie decided she was thirsty.

"Would you get me a Coke?"

"Sure you don't want to come with me?"

Josie smiled but shook her head. "I don't want to miss a play."

"One Coke coming up. Want to come, Cassandra?"

The girl shook her head, eyes fixed on Kat as she played shortstop. Josie loved watching Kat play that position. Normally, a taller, more athletic guy played there, but Kat played like she had springs on her shoes. Art pouted and pulled Josie to her feet. "We'll be back in a minute, Cassandra."

The girl didn't seem to notice, as she stayed fixed on the action. Mother motioned that she'd take care of Cassandra. Art grabbed Josie's hand and tucked her against his side while they walked.

The line at concessions was several people deep when they reached it. The gent in front of them kept looking over his shoulder and shaking his head.

"Have you ever seen anything so ridiculous?"

Art looked at the man. "Were you talking to me?"

"No, but you'll do. What are they thinking, letting a girl play?"

"Probably that she's good enough." Josie didn't try to keep the snap from her voice. Insolent man to question Kat's playing.

"Nah." The man swatted a paper through the air. "I bet her father's sponsored the team or her boyfriend's captain."

Art shook his head. "Nope. Kat's too young to have a guy. What's your name?"

He stuck out his hand. "Jack Raymond. I'm only here because my editor sent me. Seems he thinks a small tourney like this has a story buried somewhere." A sour expression twisted the young man's face. "I am definitely not cut out for this kind of sports reporting."

"Stick around, Jack, and I'll introduce you to that girl. She could very well be your story."

The thin man clamped a pencil between his teeth. "Maybe, but I can't see it."

Josie bit her lip to keep from making a retort. Kat's play should speak for itself. If the reporter didn't know that by now, then he hadn't watched the game at all.

The line moved forward again and it was Jack's turn to order. Art nodded at the window. "Go ahead."

"Dames aren't supposed to play baseball. Anyone in their right mind knows that." Jack looked toward the field. "Though she is a cute thing."

Josie hoped this Jack Raymond wouldn't take Art up on his offer to introduce him to Kat. Kat wouldn't hesitate in taking on each of his ridiculous comments.

"Well, back to the salt mines. I've got a story to file." He tipped an imaginary hat. "Nice to meet you."

Josie watched him saunter off. An unsettled feeling flared. It was a good thing he wouldn't stick around to meet Kat. She didn't need someone like him telling her not to play with the boys. It brought too much joy to Kat. Yep, they'd all be better served without Kat and Jack meeting.

sixteen

Art hurried to turn the corner and tear down the hall. He wanted to yell, "I'm late, I'm late, for a very important date." People stepped out of his way without a word from him. They must see the panic that leaked from his mind to his face. He skidded to a stop outside the conference room. It would only make things worse to run in. He steeled himself and opened the door.

When Art walked into the room, E. K. Fine III sat at the head of the conference table. "Nice of you to join us, Wilson."

Uh-oh. Never a good sign when Fine called someone out in front of everyone.

"You're in time to fill us in on your scheme to have this fine company produce airplanes."

How did the man do it? How did he call his company a fine one without cracking a smile? The company was a fine Fine company?

Charlie Sloan patted the chair next to his and removed his notebook from it. As Art took the seat, Charlie whispered, "Focus, Art."

Good advice. Art sucked in a breath. "What would you like to know, sir?"

"Why should this company manufacture plane parts?"

"I don't recommend we transition now. No, we plan, determine what changes are needed to the plant and our process. But for now, continue to craft pianos."

"Know any experts on manufacturing plane parts?"

"No, sir. I'm an accountant. I deal with numbers, not processes or manufacturing." Though the challenge of anticipating the future and plotting a course of action captured his mind. He and Charlie had spent hours elaborating on

Art's initial idea. On paper, it looked like the company could transition to plane parts with relative ease. Art excelled at his job when Fine let him focus his energy on accounting. But he knew the company's small reserve of cash would evaporate in a few months if they didn't develop a plan. It wasn't the books' fault the company stood in danger. A well-managed company should be more in the black, but that hadn't happened here. As the reality of the company's situation had emerged, he'd wondered if he should look for another job. Art didn't want to worry Josie, but he also didn't want to run the risk of unemployment.

Charlie jumped in, followed by other employees. Art relaxed as attention was diverted from him. No doubt about it. It was time to look for another position.

❧

"Cassandra. We need to hurry, honey." Josie slipped on an earring, and then examined her reflection one last time. When Annabelle had called to see if Cassandra would participate in this October program to raise awareness of the needs of children in England, it had sounded like a great idea. A few children from Canton would participate, making it a good way for Cassie to see some of her compatriots. But now that Josie raced to get Cassandra to the community meeting in time, she wondered.

"Sweetie, we have to leave now or we'll be late." No response. Josie hurried from her room. Cassandra had shut and locked her door. Josie twisted the doorknob a couple times to no avail. She rattled the doorknob, but Cassandra ignored her. "Young lady, let me in your room now."

"No."

"You'll miss the program."

"I don't care." Cassandra's pitch rose with each word. "I don't want to go somewhere where you'll show me off like a prize pet." Panic laced her words.

Josie leaned against the door. "I don't understand, Cassie."

"You want people to think you're an amazing person.

'Look at me, I took in a kid whose parents didn't want her anymore.'"

There was the rub. "Your parents love you. You'll get letters soon."

"No, I won't. I haven't received one since I arrived."

"That doesn't mean they don't love you. Or that we feel like we have to keep you. We also don't want you here so we can show you off. You're Art's cousin, part of our family. We want you with us."

Cassandra's sobs vibrated through the door.

"Let me in. We don't have to go to the program. They'll understand. But you must talk to me."

They missed the program. Josie decided if it were important, there would be future opportunities. Instead, they walked the neighborhood, ending at the library. Miss Adelaide lit up when she saw them.

"My two favorite people in the world. I declare it's good to see the two of you. Where have you kept yourselves?"

Josie shook her head slightly. No need to go backward. "We're doing okay today. Miss Adelaide, how are things here?"

"I'm swamped. Tell me you'll stay and help." Miss Adelaide rested her chin on her steepled fingers. "I can tell the kids are back in school. They all need expert advice on class projects."

Cassandra seemed willing, so they spent a few hours at the library. Cassandra pitched in to help file the books and soon returned to her usual sunny mood. On their way home, Josie gave Cassandra a quarter and let her select some candy at the drugstore.

"Thank you for the sweets."

"You're welcome." If only life's challenges could be solved with a quarter and handful of sweets. Josie absently rubbed her stomach as they finished the walk home. Cassandra ran ahead of her as she climbed the stairs to the apartment. Doris caught her eye as they walked by. Doris's eyes softened. She pulled a handkerchief out of her housecoat pocket and pressed it into Josie's hand. Josie looked at the square of cloth, puzzled.

"Thank you, Doris, but why do I need this?"

"Check your cheeks, dear." Her smile seemed watery. "I'll be up in a moment."

Josie nodded, then mounted the last stairs. Each took more effort, and by the time she reached the apartment door, she felt like she couldn't breathe. She felt overwhelmed and didn't know whether to cry it out or stifle the tears. She pressed her hand to her mouth and stared at her wedding ring.

Her throat constricted, and she groped her way to the couch, where she collapsed. A sense of panic filled her. Where had this come from? By the time Doris let herself in, Josie wasn't sure she could breathe anymore.

Doris tsked as she took off her sweater and rummaged through the cupboards. "I'll make some tea."

Josie tried to nod through her tears. "What happened?" The words slipped between hiccups.

"I'm not 100 percent sure, but I think your grief is back."

Josie shook her head. "That can't be. I've been fine."

Doris slipped into the room and settled next to Josie on the couch. "The loss you've experienced comes and goes. Some days you won't cry because of your loss. Other days it will be all you can do to move. Today must be one of your sad days."

"But I was okay until, I don't know, it hit me."

Doris wrapped her in a hug while the tears flowed unchecked. Eventually, Josie became aware that Cassandra stood at the end of the room, fear cloaking her face. Doris followed Josie's gaze.

"Cassandra, how would you like to come downstairs with me and help me bake some cookies? Mr. Duncan keeps telling me he wants some snickerdoodles for the grocery, but I need some help. How about it?"

Cassandra looked from Josie to Doris and back. Josie pushed a watery smile on her face. "It's all right with me. I'll be here whenever you're done."

"Okay. I'd like to come help."

"Be back in time to finish homework."

Cassandra rolled her eyes in the way only children can. Then she skipped to her room and put on her shoes before following Doris down the stairs. Josie watched them leave, then moved to her room. She clutched a pillow across her stomach, as if bracing herself. She tried to identify what she felt the need to brace from, but couldn't. Instead, an unsettled feeling seeped in.

Something was about to change. And she didn't think it had anything to do with her baby. Whatever it was, she couldn't shake it.

She curled up on her bed. Tried to form a prayer. All that came out was, "Father, please help."

seventeen

Mrs. Wilson,
   Would you please come to school to meet with me tomorrow?
We need to discuss Cassandra.

                                                        Miss Taylor

Josie stared at the note she'd found under Cassandra's bed. It looked like it had fallen out of her bag and lain there forgotten for a week. Miss Taylor would think she was an uninvolved, uncaring foster parent. She rubbed a hand over the ache drilling her forehead. She wanted to believe the note meant they needed to discuss good things, but the tightness in her stomach warned that wasn't the case.

Each day that passed without word from home, Cassandra pulled further inside herself. While she'd never been the most outgoing child, she'd blossomed in the months since arriving. Now she'd retreated as if protecting herself.

Without letters from home, Cassandra feared the worst. Josie couldn't blame her. Since letters hadn't made it, Josie decided to take a proactive approach. She'd send a telegram and see if Annabelle could pass the word through her work.

Reaching the decision, Josie stood and changed out of her cleaning outfit into a nice dress. She carefully applied rouge and a touch of lipstick. Pulling on pumps and pinning on a hat, she grabbed her purse and headed out the door. Maybe she could catch Miss Taylor over lunch, explain she'd found the note today.

Josie walked the few blocks to the school. She entered the doors and wound through the halls to the fourth-grade classroom. When she peeked through the door, she found the room empty. Books were scattered across the surface of the desks, and the chalkboard was covered with division and multiplication problems.

What sounded like hundreds of feet pounded off the floor. Josie looked up to see a class headed her way. None of the children looked familiar until she spotted Cassandra, standing a head shorter than the other children, with the hint of a Mona Lisa smile teasing her features.

Miss Taylor led the way. A thin woman, she struck Josie as a person who enjoyed her charges. Maybe even delighted in her work.

A cautious smile curved Miss Taylor's lips. "Mrs. Wilson."

"Hello." Josie played with her purse straps. "I'm sorry I haven't stopped by earlier. I located the note this morning."

A light—could it be relief—flickered in Miss Taylor's eyes. "Let me get the class settled, and I'll have a minute."

"Thank you." Josie smiled at Cassandra as the children walked into the classroom. The girl avoided her eyes and shuffled after the other children. Josie leaned against the wall while she waited. She had to establish contact with Cassandra's family.

Father, give me insight into her heart. Show me what to do. And give me the same for Art. Something's happening there that I don't understand. She turned over her worries and fears while she waited.

Her eyes were closed when the door opened. Josie pushed off the wall and watched Miss Taylor.

"I've got a few minutes but will have to keep a watch on the students."

"Of course."

"Cassandra's struggling."

Josie nodded. "I've noticed the shadow of a change at home, too. Is she keeping up academically?"

"Yes. I'd move her up another grade, but she's struggling so with the children right now that I don't think it would be best for her."

"Could the problem be that she's not challenged?"

Miss Taylor shook her head. "She is a little girl who is afraid."

"Do you have any recommendations?" Josie nibbled on a nail.

"I'm not a social worker, but something has to happen. Cassandra's miserable. And we have to make a change. I'm concerned she's making enemies."

"Does she still refuse to say the pledge?"

"No. She's just quiet, and that's okay." Miss Taylor shrugged. "We'll deal with that later. This is more important." Miss Taylor straightened her skirt and turned as if to go back in the classroom. "Maybe see if there are other evacuated children around here that she can get together with. Maybe knowing she's not alone will make a difference."

"Thank you," Josie whispered as Miss Taylor returned to her classroom.

Josie marched to the telegraph office and sent a message to Cassandra's parents, begging them to send some word to Cassie. She walked home and asked to use the phone. While she didn't like asking Annabelle for help—she'd helped raise Kat, after all, and that girl was turning out well—Josie knew she couldn't take care of this situation on her own.

The thought of Kat covered from head to toe in dirt but grinning so big her face just about cracked warmed Josie. Maybe Cassandra needed a good romp in a mud puddle. Art didn't seem to need much from Josie right now. She didn't have a baby. What she did have was an eight-year-old who'd retreated into a world of pain.

Josie dialed Annabelle's number and left a message. She spent the balance of the afternoon praying for Cassie. As soon as the girl got home, she ran to her room and slammed the door. Wails echoed through the apartment. Josie looked at the door, then approached it. She resisted asking what was wrong. Cassie's answer would be nothing, but the slammed door said something else.

"Cassandra, I've got cookies and milk ready for you. Fresh from the oven."

Silence answered her.

"I'll bring some to you."

"Thank you." The muffled words sounded watery.

Josie went to the kitchen and brought a plate with several chocolate chip cookies and a tall glass of milk to Cassie's room. She opened the door. "Here you go, sweetie."

Cassandra looked at her with watery eyes. "Am I in trouble?"

"No. I want to help you. I'm so sorry you're not happy. Is there something I can do to help?"

Cassandra's chin quivered. "I want to go home. I want to see my mum and hug my grandmum."

"I wish I could do that for you."

"It was my birthday yesterday, and nobody knew."

A rock settled in Josie's stomach. How could she have forgotten to learn such an important date?

❧

Art sat in the unexpected meeting, curious about why E. K. Fine had called it. His normal pattern was to head home as soon after noon as possible on Fridays. Instead, it was four thirty, and he'd called a full staff meeting of non-plant employees.

"Know what this is about, Art?" Stan plopped onto the chair next to him and crossed his legs and arms.

"No. I bet Charlie does."

Charlie laughed. "I don't have the pulse of the company like that. We'll learn together."

That worried Art. E.K. acting outside his normal patterns seemed a red flag. The guy didn't like to put in one extra minute of work. He enjoyed resting on the laurels of his father and grandfather. Maybe that's why Grandfather had adamantly refused to help Art. Wanted to keep him from getting lazy on the money others accumulated.

More employees filtered in until there was standing room only. The air turned stale and hot. Art pulled at his shirt collar. Someone along the wall opened a couple windows, but even the crisp October air didn't help much. More ties and bowties got loosened.

E.K. swaggered into the room, and Art sat straighter in his chair.

"Attention." The murmur of voices drowned out E.K. He clapped to little avail. Art whistled through his fingers. The piercing sound caused the conversations to die. "Thank you." E.K. placed his hands on the table in front of him. "I've called you here for a quick meeting. Our family has decided to sell this company." Murmuring rose from around the room. E.K. waved them down. "I am pleased to announce that we have a purchaser and a signed agreement. I wanted you to hear from me before rumors circulated. The Wilson Holding Company out of Dayton has acquired us."

Art could see E.K.'s mouth continue to move, but nothing registered. All he heard translated into static. Grandfather had bought the company? Why? The family had never done anything related to manufacturing musical instruments. It seemed far outside the investment parameters Grandfather had developed.

Art knew from working on the books things weren't as solid as E.K. wanted everyone to believe. But this? He tried to relax his shoulders, but he wanted to leave.

This could not be good news for him. Not when Grandfather had made it so clear he was not impressed with Art's choice of employer or position.

"It's my pleasure to introduce the man who will soon own this great company."

Art watched as Grandfather strode into the room. His suit was fully buttoned, and a precisely folded handkerchief was tucked in the pocket. With his silver hair and mahogany walking stick, Grandfather looked ready to take on anything the company could throw his way.

Art swallowed and wished he'd chosen a seat toward the back. There was no way Grandfather would overlook him. Nope. Grandfather located him immediately, his frown lightening a moment before returning.

"Good afternoon." Grandfather's rich voice filled the

conference room. "My company is interested in this company because I see great potential here. It will be up to each of you to prove that you have the ability to contribute to its growth. I am not interested in employees who maintain the status quo." His stare bored through Art. "That will be all."

Grandfather turned on his heel and left the room. Art watched him leave. Why not stay long enough to say hi? There must be some event back in Dayton, though Grandfather would be hard pressed to make it home in time for anything tonight.

E.K. clapped his hands. "That will be all."

Some people left the room as if they couldn't wait to leave. Others gathered in small groups around the periphery. Art remained in his seat until he felt a sharp jab in his ribs.

"What are you waiting for, Wilson? Let's get the weekend started." Stan waggled his eyebrows and made a drinking motion.

Some folks couldn't take no for an answer. "No, thanks. I've got some work to finish, and then it's home for me."

"I'll drink one for you." Stan strutted from the room.

Charlie shook his head as he watched the man leave. "Someday, his behavior will catch up with him."

Much as Art might like to believe it, he had a feeling Stan was like a cat who always landed on his feet. "I've got to get a project wrapped up. See you next week."

Art stumbled into the office and sank into his chair. He laid his head against the back, eyes closed, as he tried to wipe fear from his mind. Grandfather had not bought the company just to put him on edge. No, Grandfather was a businessman who carefully investigated potential companies. He'd seen something that made the company look like a good investment, one that happened to employ Art.

Art looked at the stack of ledgers on his desk, then shook his head. No way his mind would focus enough to finish them accurately tonight. Time to go home and forget about work. He had to before he drove himself crazy trying to anticipate what Grandfather would do once he officially owned the company. Art grabbed his swagger coat and bolted from the office.

He needed some space. Grandfather had made it clear the last time they visited that he wanted Art to stand on his own two feet. How did buying the company Art worked for figure into that independence unless Grandfather wanted to teach him something?

eighteen

From the moment he walked in the door, Art had mumbled to himself and slammed doors. Josie watched, unsure what to do. He threw his briefcase on the floor, then tossed his coat across the back of the davenport. Tugging at his tie, he stomped to their bedroom.

Cassandra had yet to emerge from her room. Now this.

It would be another delightful evening in their home unless she could get to the bottom of what bothered Art. She determined to control what she could: her attitude. She'd start there and hope it spread throughout the apartment.

"*A mighty fortress is our God.*" She hummed the tune over and over, building to a crescendo before easing into a popular tune. Before long, she transitioned to another hymn. Peace and joy washed over her as she focused on her heavenly Father.

She inhaled. The rich scent of meatloaf and potatoes filled the air. She grabbed hot pads and pulled the pan from the oven. Soon the meatloaf, along with peas, baked potatoes, and bread waited on the table. Art still hadn't returned from the bedroom, so she finished setting the table. She lit a couple of tapers and watched the flames' reflections dance across the surface of the glasses. It had been awhile since she'd decorated the table with care like this, and she liked the effect. Once the meatloaf had a chance to set, she cut it.

Neither Art nor Cassandra exited their lairs based on the aroma, so she went after them. She knocked on Cassandra's door, then slipped it open. Cassandra lay curled on her side, doll tucked under her arm, mouth open as she slept. The girl's cheeks were puffy and streaked with wetness. The child must be exhausted to have fallen asleep already. Josie decided to let her sleep. She grabbed the blanket from the foot of the bed and pulled it over Cassandra.

Josie left the room and opened the door to her bedroom. Art sat on the edge, dress shirt off, head in his hands. Her heart raced at the sight.

"Art." She hurried to his side. "What's wrong?"

"I don't know for sure."

She frowned. That didn't make much sense. "Are you ill? Did you get fired?"

He kept answering no to her questions, but he wouldn't look at her.

"Art Wilson. You are scaring me. It's time for dinner. Cassandra's asleep, so we can talk over meatloaf." She tugged on his hands until he groaned and stood. She pulled a face. "My meatloaf's not that bad."

He laughed, the sound fractured and edgy, but an improvement. "Lead on, Mrs. Wilson."

"Thank you. I think I will after you put something on over your T-shirt." Art complied, and they settled at the table. After Art said a quick grace, she studied him. "What's happened?"

"I'm probably blowing everything out of proportion."

"It's easy to do."

"Grandfather's bought E. K. Fine's Piano Company."

Josie's fork clattered to her plate. "Really? Why?"

"That precise question has worried me since I learned it late this afternoon. Fine isn't the typical company Grandfather purchases. It's not a natural fit for his portfolio." Art leaned over his plate. "All I can come up with is that he either wants to monitor me or take this job away from me."

"Art Wilson, that is the craziest thing I've ever heard. Why would your grandfather wish to see you jobless? He loves you and only wants what's best for you."

"See, I know you're right, but another part of me—"

"He does care, you know. He shows it through pushing you to be your best. That works for him."

"But it leaves me worried at times like this."

"You don't need to be. Why not give him the benefit of the doubt? Maybe he investigated the company after learning you'd accepted the job. Needed to make sure it was good enough for you or something. Through that research, he decided it needed someone who could improve the company. Maybe he wouldn't normally take any notice, but because you work here, he does."

Art nodded, his fingers tracing the pattern in the table-cloth. "That makes sense."

"So don't worry about it." Josie placed her hand over his, stilling its restless motion. "Work hard for him. He'll be pleased." She squeezed, then released his hand. The meatloaf smelled wonderful, and she served each of them a slice.

Art took a few bites. Josie let him eat in quiet, giving him the time to process his concerns.

"Mrs. Wilson, you are a wonderful woman."

"I am?"

"Yes." Art scooted his plate back and stretched. "I'd like to take a walk, if you don't mind."

Josie looked at the table. The dishes and cleanup would keep her busy for a while. "That's fine with me. Remember, everything will be okay."

≈

Art put his coat back on, then headed downstairs and out the door. He walked with no destination in mind, letting the fresh air and exercise clear his head. He'd never thought of himself as a fearful man, yet since the move to Cincinnati, he seemed to keep one eye looking over his shoulder. He should be at ease, enjoying every moment with his new bride. Instead, he detected her disappointment in the way he didn't share every emotional valley with her over the loss of their baby. She couldn't seem to understand he'd grieved and now looked to the future.

And now this wrinkle with Grandfather.

Art's thoughts roiled until he collapsed on a bench in Eden

Park. The sky had darkened as he fought his fears. If only it felt like he'd conquered them.

God, help me. That was all he could manage. Over and over the phrase repeated in his mind.

It felt inadequate. He should craft sentences that would persuade God to shift the course of events into a vein that he liked. Instead, that one sentence repeated like a broken record bouncing through his mind, ricocheting off his fears.

He wrestled in the darkness till he felt wrung out.

Finally, he stumbled to his knees. *Father, take this weight from me. I beg You.*

Peace never really flooded. Instead, a trickle dripped over him. Gave him the opportunity to choose. So he stood and marched back to his home. God was in control of all the details of his life. He'd released those burdens. It was time to live like the burdens were gone and the future firmly established in God's hand.

A strange car sat in front of the building when Art walked up, but he barely glanced at it.

His place was inside. Climbing the stairs, he slowed when he heard voices from the third floor. Who would be in his apartment at this hour? Then he made out the visiting voice.

The rich voice belonged to Grandfather. Art sucked in a breath, then squared his shoulders. He could recover from anything Grandfather had to throw at him. He'd graduated from college, paid for it on his own, acquired skills. Used those skills successfully. He didn't know what else to do to make Grandfather proud of him.

He opened the door and waited for Grandfather to acknowledge him.

"Son." Grandfather nodded from his seat in the shell chair. He treated the seat as if it were his throne.

"Hello, Grandfather."

Josie perched on the edge of the davenport and looked from one to the other. "Your grandfather arrived awhile ago. I was making a pot of coffee. Would you like some, Art?"

Her eyes pleaded with him to be nice.

"Yes, thank you." Art stood a moment, then stripped off his coat and settled on the davenport.

"Where's our cousin?" Grandfather barked.

Josie stepped into the doorway. "She fell asleep before dinner. I doubt we'll see her before breakfast. The school week tends to wear her out. They have her in an advanced grade, you see." Josie bit her lower lip in that adorable way she had when she was nervous and talking too much.

"Hmm. Is everything working out with her?"

"Josie has done a wonderful job with Cassandra. She and Cassie have developed a good relationship. We've got a few issues to iron out with school, but even those are improved."

"Glad to hear."

A plate clattered against the counter. Art placed his elbows on his knees and steepled his fingers. "I know you've got a long drive in front of you, Grandfather. What can I do for you?"

Grandfather sighed. "I'm interested in making superior instruments."

Art guffawed. Grandfather's brows knit together at the sound. "Sorry. That's not the answer I expected."

"Obviously."

"Your companies have always focused on consumer goods. Pianos are luxury items."

"Maybe. I think the company is poised to do interesting things or fall apart. Management will play a big role in that success or lack thereof. Consider this an opportunity to prove yourself."

Josie brought in a tray loaded with her china coffee service. "I'm sorry, but I wasn't sure how you liked your coffee."

"Black is fine."

She nodded, then filled two cups with the steaming liquid.

"I have a proposition for you." Grandpa took a sip, all the while looking over the edge of the cup at Art. "I'm buying your company. It's in dire need of visionary management. I think you could provide at least a part of that. But you have to want to. So here's what I suggest. You step up and generate ideas and leadership. Do so, and you can move into management."

Josie gasped, then slapped a hand over her mouth. "Art, that sounds like a great offer."

"I'll have a couple of my most trusted employees at the plant starting on Tuesday. You'll have one month to convince them you're ready to join them." Grandfather eyed him intently as if measuring him. "I'll tell you my decision on Thanksgiving."

"All right. I accept your challenge."

Grandfather gave an approving nod. "That's my boy. Give this challenge everything you've got. I think you're ready to succeed. Wouldn't be here if I thought anything else. I'll see myself out."

Art stood and offered a hand, but Grandfather wrapped him in a quick hug. "Josephine."

"Good night, Grandfather."

After Grandfather left, Art stood by the window. He watched the man climb into the backseat of his vehicle. The chauffer Art hadn't noticed when he walked up started the car and drove away. Grandfather's challenge echoed through his mind. *Be management-ready in four weeks.* As he considered all that Grandfather expected of his team, Art knew he couldn't prepare in such a short period.

As always, Grandfather had set him up with a chance to prove himself.

Ultimately, as with most challenges Grandfather issued, he had no choice. Sink or swim. Thrive or fail. Grandfather didn't care which.

nineteen

Sunday morning, Josie got Cassandra ready for church while Art scrambled eggs. The morning felt relaxed as they ate breakfast and brushed teeth, then pulled on light coats.

Josie inhaled deeply as they stepped outside. The air felt crisp, the kind of day that made Josie think of apple pie with crumb topping. She could almost smell cinnamon in the air. Art linked his arm through hers, and they walked to church. Doris and Scott stood on the steps, greeting people. Cassandra ran to Doris for a hug, and Josie smiled at the sight. No, the child wasn't with her family, but they'd crafted a community for her here in Cincinnati.

The organist played a prelude as Art led them to seats in the back. Josie soaked in the music and the peace. The sweet sense of God's presence stayed with her through the hymns and into the sermon. Art shifted next to her. What brought her peace seemed to agitate him that morning.

After lunch, Art stomped around the apartment while Cassandra curled on the davenport, ignoring him with her nose buried in a book. Lucy Maud Montgomery's tales of Anne of Green Gables had captured the girl's imagination. Josie was glad to see the child engrossed.

"Art, please stop pacing. You're going to worry Doris." Josie blew a curl out of her eyes. "Trust me, you don't want her up here. She's tenacious when she thinks there's a problem." She'd meant the words to tease.

He clomped to a stop. "I don't need you telling me what I do wrong." He turned away, muttering, "I get enough of that at work."

Josie sank into a chair at the dining room table. "I'm sorry. I didn't mean it that way. Want to tell me about work? I tend to assume everything's fine since you don't mention it much."

Art looked at Cassandra, then at Josie. "Can we take a walk?"

"Yes, I'll just knock on Doris's door on our way out. Cassie, we're going outside for a bit. Let Mrs. Duncan know if you need anything, okay?"

The girl nodded, never pulling her nose from the book.

Instead of keeping an eye on the door for Cassandra, Doris headed toward the stairs. "I can relax up there just as well as down here. Go enjoy this beautiful day."

"Thank you. We won't be too long."

"Take your time. There's no rush."

Josie hugged Doris, then followed Art down the stairs. His long stride left her stretching to keep up. After a block, she stopped. Art continued a few feet before he turned.

"What?"

"Wondering if you'd like to slow your steps so I can keep up." Josie smiled at him. "I'd love to walk with you but don't feel up for a run."

A sheepish look cloaked Art's face. "I'm sorry, Josie. Guess I let my thoughts push me." He walked back to her and offered his hand. "Would you like to walk with me?"

Josie held her tongue as they walked another block. She'd learned Art sometimes needed to process what he thought before sharing it. This seemed one of those times. She prayed for him—prayed that God would shower him with peace and wisdom, that whatever bothered him would fall into proper perspective.

Art ran his fingers through his closely cropped hair. "Things are changing at the company. Each day I'm under scrutiny."

"Why do you think that?"

"Grandfather's spies are everywhere, but it's impossible to know what I do that pleases or upsets Grandfather."

"He loves you, Art."

"Probably, but he's always insisted I stand on my own. That was easier to do when he was at a distance. Now he's there.

At my job. It's almost enough to make me hunt for a new position."

"You could."

"But I can't surrender before I try. I have to prove I am capable. I can succeed."

"You don't have to prove it to me. I know you're a wonderful man. I wouldn't have married you otherwise." Josie watched him carefully. "Tell me what happened this week."

"One of Grandpa's watchers found a problem with the corporate books."

That could be bad. "Was it your work?"

"No. Several entries made over the months before we arrived. But I didn't find them. Didn't think to look for them. Grandpa will say I'm too trusting. Don't have the bull-dogged determination it takes."

Josie wanted to kiss the lines from his face. Remind him how very much she loved him. "I love you, Mr. Wilson."

He squeezed her hand. "I love you, too."

At the end of the block, they turned to head back to the apartment. Art looked more relaxed, though Josie couldn't pinpoint why. Maybe the act of sharing the burden was enough.

The next morning after Art had left for work and Cassandra was ensconced at school, Annabelle stopped by the apartment. Her sleek blond hair bobbed at her chin, and her tailored clothing had a Katherine Hepburn style. Josie tucked loose strands of hair behind her ears and wished she'd taken a few more minutes on her appearance before the social worker arrived.

"Has Cassandra improved?" Annabelle leaned forward in her seat, gaze locked on Josie.

"We still haven't heard from her family. Cassandra is doing well in school, and keeps her chin up most of the time. But there are times, usually at night, where she thinks about them and worries. I'd hoped you would hear something. Our wire didn't produce anything. Do you have word or another idea on how to reach them? Is there anything we can do to find out if they're safe? I think the not knowing is what bothers her."

Annabelle made a note. "I'll keep trying. I'm not surprised she's homesick. These kids have been taken from their homes and sent too far away. The Battle of Britain is too intense to send them home, though. Then we've got parents like Cassandra's whom we can't locate."

"Does that mean something's happened to them?" Josie didn't think Cassandra could handle that. What child could?

"Oh no. It just means war conditions are in place. I bet we'll hear from them soon, and Cassandra's fears will be quieted." Annabelle flipped a page in the file. "How's she doing making friends?"

"Cassie is a delight with adults. She's showering hugs and seems attached to more than Art and me. But she's isolated at school. She still won't say the pledge, which doesn't help. It reminds the others that she's different each day, beyond the accent." The teakettle whistled, and Josie jumped up from the davenport. "Would you like some tea?"

"Yes." Annabelle didn't look up from her file, where she wrote notes. Josie wished she could see the words.

She slipped into the kitchen and pulled the tea together. Annabelle hadn't come to find fault with them. So why did it feel like the social worker could decide this placement had failed and take Cassandra from them? Her fears were running wild again. This child had entered her family, and Josie needed her. The corner of her heart ready to mother loved caring for Cassandra. And without the girl, the grief might explode again. A shudder coursed through Josie at the thought.

Now was not the time to allow the grief to well up again. After Annabelle left, Josie could fall on her face and beg God for answers. She should have done that first. Annabelle might have ideas, but God would have the perfect solution.

Josie loaded a tray with her Grandmother's china teapot,

two porcelain teacups, and a plate of snickerdoodles she'd baked with Cassandra that weekend. "Do you like sugar with your tea?"

"Yes, and cream, too."

"Ah, you like it the British way."

"I suppose all the time with the evacuees has influenced my tastes."

Josie poured a cup for each of them, adding cream to Annabelle's, then settled back on the couch. "Annabelle, I would like any suggestions you have. Cassandra means too much to me to not do everything I can to help her."

"Could you bring her to Canton for a weekend? Maybe having her around other children from back home would help."

"I'll have to talk to Art about that. It's such a long drive." Josie chewed on a fingernail as she considered the logistics. "We can talk and see if that's something Cassandra would like."

"There are certain times when the Hoover Company has planned excursions for the children. I'll let you know when those come up. I'm sure they wouldn't mind adding Cassandra to the mix." Annabelle blew on her tea before taking a sip. "As long as she's happy here, we're fine. And it sounds like she's doing well overall. On school, see if there's a girl or two she'd like to have over after school. Help facilitate that relationship. It could make a world of difference for her to feel like she has a few friends. I'm sure several of the girls think she's practically exotic coming from overseas."

"Thank you." As the social worker gathered her things and left, Josie felt a surge of energy. Time to help Cassandra make the last transition and find friends her age.

Josie fell to her knees beside the couch. *Father, help me focus on things that will make a difference to Cassandra. I want to be someone You can use in her life. Grant me insight into her heart and thoughts.* Her prayers flowed for a long time until she felt release. Then they shifted to Art and his job.

When she stood, she brushed tears from her face and headed to the kitchen. Time to show Cassandra how much she cared for her.

Minutes before Cassandra would walk in the door from school, Josie pulled a pan of fresh cookies out of the oven. As a child, she'd loved walking into a home that smelled of baking and sitting down to a tall glass of milk and Mother's latest creation. Mark, Kat, and she had often fought over who got the last cookie, with Mark winning. Maybe Cassandra needed the same opportunity to unwind from the stress of school. And it didn't matter that they'd just made cookies that weekend. There was something in the aroma of cookies that helped one unwind.

Maybe during that time, Josie could help steer Cassandra toward appropriate actions.

Dirt and wetness streaked Cassandra's cheeks and clothes when she walked in the door.

"What happened?"

Cassandra tried to walk past her, but Josie stopped her. She placed a hand on Cassandra's cheek and brushed at the grime. "I need to know what happened."

"Nothing." Her shoulders slumped, but anger or tears tinged Cassandra's words. Josie studied her but couldn't tell which caused the veneer surrounding the child.

"Cassie, 'nothing' is not an answer. Something happened, and you need to tell me."

"You're not my mother." Cassandra stomped her foot. Okay, so it was anger in her voice.

"If it involves you, I need to know. Especially since it involves school." Josie put an arm around Cassandra and led her stiff form to the table. "And you're going to do it while we eat fresh cookies and drink some milk."

Cassandra's edges softened. She let Josie lead her, then took a bite of the cookie. Before Josie could stop her, she inhaled four more cookies. The poor child acted like she hadn't eaten a meal in days.

"Did you not like lunch today?" She'd packed a simple lunch of a peanut butter sandwich, apple, and a cupcake.

Cassandra's chin quivered. "I don't know."

"Why not?" Josie feared she knew the answer before she heard it.

"Somebody took it from me." A tear streaked its way through the grime on her cheek.

"Has this happened before?"

Cassandra nodded. "He told me he'd beat me up if I told. Then today, he pushed me on the way home. I scraped my knee." Cassandra held up her knee, and Josie leaned in to kiss it.

"Oh, Cassie. I'm so sorry. Has he pushed you before?"

Cassandra shook her head.

"Good. Did you eat at school at all this week?"

Heat spiraled through Josie's body as the child shook her head. No wonder she'd had some trouble. She hadn't eaten lunch in who knew how long. This she could handle.

"Okay. I'll go to school with you tomorrow and talk to Miss Taylor." Cassandra's eyes got big as saucers. "Don't worry. I won't make you say who is doing this to you, though I'd certainly like to. You shouldn't be bullied."

"If it's not me, it'll be one of the smaller children."

Josie eyed Cassandra. How a child that petite could be concerned about smaller children! "Why did this boy start picking on you?"

"I wanted to play kickball with the boys in the class. He said I couldn't, but others let me on a team. I beat him." She shrugged. "I guess he's not used to losing."

Josie had to stifle a smile. Yet another way Cassandra mirrored Kat.

When Art arrived home an hour later, Cassandra still sat at the table with Josie, working on a puzzle. Josie hadn't wanted to leave the table when Cassandra settled in to spend time with her. Josie scrambled out of her chair. "I'm sorry, Art. I haven't started dinner."

twenty

So this was what it felt like to have one's future completely outside their control. Art wrestled with the eighty-pound weight that dogged his steps. Most days he could leave it outside the door when he came home. Today, it followed him inside.

The sight of Josie and Cassandra working a puzzle on the table eased the burden.

"How was your day?" Josie's smile warmed his heart.

"Another day at the office."

Cassandra looked up, puzzle piece held in one hand. "Dad used to say that all the time. Before the war."

Art rumpled her curls. "He'll say it again after the British sweep the Germans back behind their borders."

She frowned at him. "Don't lie to me."

"I didn't mean to." When did she become a little adult? "Anyway, I'm starved. What will you ladies prepare?"

"Grilled cheese and soup. Simple is the order of the day." Josie pushed back from the table but laid another piece in the puzzle as she stood. "I think this may yet shape into something. Cassandra, what's your guess?"

Cassandra eyed the misshapen image. So many gaps remained, Art wondered that she even attempted to determine how it would look.

"The Statute of Liberty?"

Art studied the lines of blues and slashes of gray. Maybe she had it.

"Great guess. I told you we'd get there." Josie pulled the puzzle box lid from under her chair. "Maybe this will help us after all."

"Will you help me, Art?" Cassandra's soft brown eyes pleaded with him.

How could he say no?

He settled at the table and watched her a moment.

"You have to do more than watch."

"Of course. But you have to show me the box. I can't do it without a picture. Not the prize puzzle-maker you are."

She laughed and pulled it from under the table. "Don't show me."

"All right." He studied the photo of the Statute of Liberty and groaned. The colors were so similar. "I have to warn you, I'm terrible at puzzles. Always mess them up."

"How?" She looked as if she didn't believe him.

"Putting the wrong pieces together. My mother always accused me of forcing pieces to match that weren't supposed to." He picked up a red piece and crammed it next to a light blue one.

"Now I see." Cassandra separated the pieces. "Maybe you should watch."

Josie's soft chuckle tickled his ear. He looked up to find her standing next to his chair with a plate of food. "Here are some appetizers for the puzzle-piecers."

"Thanks. I think Cassandra's right." He jammed another couple of pieces together. "My role may be to cheer her on."

"No. I think you should sort them all by color." A mischievous light filled Cassandra's eyes. As he considered the mishmash of pieces, he understood why. It would take someone a year to sort the tiny pieces into the correct piles.

He tweaked her nose, and she squealed.

❧

"So what's with the old man?" Stan rolled his chair closer to Art's desk.

Art tried to ignore Stan and the fact Grandfather strolled the halls of E. K. Fine's Piano Company again today. Didn't he have a dozen other companies to run?

"Didn't mean to get you all worked up with that question." Stan put his hand up, palm out, in front of him. "I'll head on back to my desk. My ledgers." His chair wheels squeaked in protest.

After a deep breath, Art pinched his nose and tried to think. He grabbed his mug and took a gulp, then sputtered as the steamy bitter liquid burned his tongue and throat.

Charlie glanced up from the work spread on top of his desk. "You okay?"

Art shook his head as he tried to breathe. Charlie jumped up to help, and Art held up a hand to stop him. "Scorched my mouth."

"All right?"

"I will be." Art set the mug down and watched Grandfather enter the office. "Why do you think he's here again?"

"Determining whether you're ready for more."

Stan snorted. "And pianos are perfectly matched to his investment strategy."

"I don't know. Grandfather usually leaves tours to others." But his grandson didn't work at other companies.

"Here comes the big cheese." Stan sounded a little too chipper. What did he have up his sleeve?

"Good morning, gentlemen." Grandfather's gaze stopped on Art and a faint smile tweaked his face. Art felt Charlie watching him with questions growing by the moment. Grandfather allowed E.K. to introduce him to a few employees. He stopped at Art's desk. "Art. How are Josie and Cassandra?"

"Fine, sir."

"Good. I'll be back after the tour."

It took effort to force his thoughts to the task the company paid him to do, but he eventually marshaled his mind to the streams of data. Soon he was immersed in the numbers, sorting out and anticipating problems.

A shadow fell over his desk and he looked up. Grandfather stood over him.

"I'd like a word with you." While phrased as a request, Grandfather left no question this was not an offer Art could avoid.

"I can take a short break."

Grandfather leaned on his cane a bit as they walked down

the hall and into a vacant office. "Sit."

Art sank on the edge of a chair as Grandfather stood over him. "My sources have told me about the projects you're working on. You've done well, but you could do more."

"I haven't been here a year." Art clamped his mouth shut.

"Art, you have the potential to be more than a bookkeeper, but you have to think and act like a manager."

Art wiped a hand over his face. "I expect that will take time. I know I'm new. I'm learning all I can and hope to be promoted in time."

"Humor me. Show me what you can do. Not everyone is willing to work. But that's what's needed to stand out from everyone else." Grandfather leaned forward. "You got that fancy college education. Put it to work. And not simply by making sure numbers are in the correct column. There's much more you could do."

Art caught the challenge in his grandfather's eyes. "All right. What do you expect?"

"To see how far you'll push yourself. How hard you'll work. Instincts. . .they can't be taught."

Art couldn't make heads or tails out of the innuendo Grandfather expected him to understand. But he saw the challenge and was ready to tackle it. He'd work hard, show Grandfather what he'd learned. And some day, he'd move up.

❧

Josie looked at the invitation. With a flick of her wrist, she added a flower to the corner. There. Now it looked perfect.

She'd grown tired of the feeling she couldn't help Art with his job, so she'd decided to do something about it. Charlie's wife, Diane, had jumped in to help her compile a list of the wives of the managers and others in Art's department. Josie thought a tea would serve as an opportunity to get to know them and learn more about the company. While Art had worked there for almost a year, Josie didn't know much about it at all. Now, family owned the company.

She looked at the stack of envelopes and felt excited. She'd loved helping Mama with faculty parties. She should have done this before.

Cassandra and her new friend from school, Ruth, helped her bake cookies and tarts the day before the tea. By the time they finished, Cassandra and Ruth were covered in flour, and the kitchen rang with laughter. The day of the tea, Josie spent the morning making petite egg salad sandwiches. Cucumber would have finished the table, but the season had passed. When Diane arrived an hour before the event, she arranged the treats artfully on plates.

The table didn't look right without Mama's Wedgwood china, but her simple dishes would have to do. Hopefully, the women would come for the chance to get out of the house and meet others rather than to inspect her possessions.

As the clock ticked closer to two o'clock, the butterflies took up residence in her stomach. She pressed a hand against it and moaned.

"Are you okay, Josie?" Diane looked at her, brow crinkled.

"I will be once everybody gets here."

"Even if it's a few, it will be a great start. No one's done anything like this before."

"Leave it to me to lead the way." Ugh, nausea boiled in her throat.

A light knock echoed off the door. Josie hurried to open it. A prim-looking woman in a broad-banded hat stood on the landing. "Are you Mrs. Miller?"

Josephine smiled and extended her hand. "I am. Please come in." The woman handed over her raincoat. Josie took it and gestured to her petite friend. "This is Diane Sloan."

"Pleased to meet you both." Her gray curls bobbed against the back of her neck.

Josephine opened her mouth to ask who the first woman was, when heels clicked against the stairs. She turned to find a haggard-looking woman huffing to the top of the stairs. "Stars and garters, you should warn a soul about how many stairs there are to climb." She leaned against the doorframe and fanned her face. "I'll think twice about coming again."

The first woman waved a hand in the air as if brushing a snowflake from her nose. "Don't worry about Melanie. She tends toward the dramatic."

"Josie, this fine woman is Mrs. Jonathan Allen." Diane smiled sweetly at the gray-haired woman. "And Melanie is Mrs. Josiah Trumble."

Melanie frowned at Mrs. Allen. "If I tend on the dramatic, she lands toward the cold side of things."

Josie gasped. Had Melanie really insulted her guest? This tea time would implode before it even got underway. She closed her mouth and gestured toward the sitting area. If the verbal sparring continued like this, the apartment wasn't big enough to contain everyone. "Why don't you have a seat? Can I take anyone else's coat?"

With the ease of a woman fully content in her own skin, Diane settled nerves and eased the conversation into politer veins while Josie pulled the teakettle toward the hotter part of the stove. Three more women joined them in time for the tea and treats. While the women filled their plates, Josie pulled Diane to the side.

"Remind me how each woman fits into the company."

"Mrs. Allen is the wife of the vice president. Mr. Allen is a second cousin to the Fine family. Mrs. Trumble's husband is new. He may have come with the new buyer." Diane spoke discretely, smiling serenely the entire time. "Then there's our husbands."

"I think I know what they do."

"Your challenge will be to keep Mrs. Allen happy. Rumor has it, she has the ear of her husband, and he does as he's told."

Josie threw a lemon tea cookie and tiny biscuit sandwich on her plate. The spicy mustard tickled her taste buds, and she hoped it did the same for the others. Quiet murmurs filled the edges of the room as the women enjoyed the snacks. After a bit, the women focused on Josie.

"Why did you invite us over?" Mrs. Allen's tone was light, but an edge carved through the air between them.

"I thought it would be nice to meet all of you. Our husbands work together, after all." A series of blank faces stared back at her. Was it so hard to believe she wanted to meet them? Diane gestured for her to continue. Josie swallowed. She had a good idea. Doris had loved it and encouraged her to take on the project. Surely, these women would agree.

"Cat got your tongue?" Melanie squinted at her.

"What? Um, no. Actually, I had an idea." Several women leaned away from her as if to get as far from her as possible. Josie cleared her throat. "A church in this part of town provides relief to many of the city's poor." A couple of the ladies wrinkled their noses. "Many children receive help through meals. But I thought it would be wonderful if we helped by taking on the project of ensuring each of those children receives a Christmas present and stocking."

Mrs. Allen snorted. "That's their parents' responsibility."

"Not if the parents don't have jobs."

A younger woman raised her hand. "I actually think it's a good idea. It would be fun to shop for children."

"And whose money will you use?" Mrs. Allen looked down her nose at the woman. "It doesn't sprout from the ground."

Josie tried to smile around the lump in her throat. "Art and I could contribute a bit, and I think others would, too."

Diane brought a plate of cookies around. "I've already talked to several friends from my church who would like to contribute. The children won't expect anything extravagant, after all."

"You may waste your time if you choose. However, I have other ways to waste my time." Mrs. Allen stood, back ramrod straight. "I'll take my wrap."

Josie scurried to get it for her, then watched in shock as she swept from the apartment. In quick succession, the others left. She stared after them. "What just happened?"

twenty-one

The threat of snow hung in the air as heavy gray clouds coated the sky. Art pulled the collar of his coat around his throat as he walked to the plant. The first week of November wasn't too early for the first snowstorm, but he wouldn't mind if it delayed. The wind whistled a desolate tune that matched his mood.

The uncertainty at E. K. Fine Piano Company had eased as Grandfather's managers had stepped in and Fine eased out. The transition should be complete by the new year. Not a moment too soon. Word had leaked he was related to Grandfather. With that came the expectation he knew Grandfather's plans. Nobody believed him when he denied it. If anything, common opinion had evolved to the point his colleagues thought him part of any problem that arose.

He stumbled into the building and shook his coat off. After he hung it on its hook, he sat at his desk. Grandfather might think he should do more than work with numbers, but he really liked it.

E.K. bustled through the door. "A word with you, Mr. Wilson."

Art stifled a groan. He didn't have the reserves to deal with E.K. III before a cup of coffee. He bit his tongue and began to stand. "Certainly."

After a glance around the office, he motioned Art back into his seat. "This won't take long. Some concerns have been raised about the job you're doing."

"I don't understand."

"You're placed on probation."

Art's jaw dropped. "Why?"

"Call it one of my last decisions as president of this company."

Charlie slid into the room and eyed Art.

Fine looked at Charlie then turned back to Art. "I'd encourage you to put your full effort into your position. And tell your wife to leave the other women alone."

"What?" Josie had seemed a bit upset after her tea party last week, but she hadn't said much to him about it.

"She set off Mrs. Allen. Not a wise thing to do."

This time Art couldn't stifle his groan. Of all the women to annoy, Mrs. Allen, wife of the vice president, was a doozy of a choice. "Yes, sir."

"That'll be all." E.K. practically clicked his heels together and scurried from the room.

Charlie leaned back in his chair. "What was that about?"

"Josie's little party." He ground his teeth. "Seems she forgot to tell me the full story."

"Diane didn't mention anything out of the ordinary."

"Hmph." Art couldn't wait to let Josie know that her little party had placed him on probation. What would happen to them if he lost his job? And what about Cassandra? Would she be sent to another home? He couldn't imagine Josie's reaction if she lost the child.

Art's frustration simmered below the surface throughout the day. By the time he reached the grocery, he was ready to boil. *Lord, help me keep my temper in check.* He'd need all the help he could get on that front.

The grocery stood empty, so Art walked through it to the stairs. Cassandra sat on the stairs with a book. She half-smiled at him when she saw him. Her tangled curls framed her face, and her dress could use an iron, but she looked content.

"What are you doing out here?"

"Waiting for you, Art." She clutched an envelope in her lap.

A spark of warmth spread through him. "Do I spy a letter? Is it from home?"

She smiled, revealing a gap between her teeth. "It's from my mum. She says everyone's fine." A frown threatened to darken her face. "Though the letter's three weeks old."

"But at least you received one."

"Yes, sir. Oh, Josie wanted to warn you she didn't try to start the kitchen on fire."

Art took a second look at Cassandra. The child seemed completely sincere in her statement. He bolted up the stairs. As he climbed, whiffs of smoke hung in the air. He waved a hand in front of his face.

"Josie?"

"Here." The muffled sound drifted from the kitchen. He laughed when he saw her. She'd tied a towel around her nose and mouth and looked like she wanted to join Butch Cassidy's gang.

"What happened?"

She tried to wave like nothing much, but tears streamed from her eyes. "Bacon got away from me."

He rushed to her side and grabbed her face between his hands. He turned her head from side to side as he examined what he could see of her face. "Are you okay?"

"Feeling foolish. I should be able to cook bacon without this happening." She sucked in a deep breath, then started coughing.

A surge of relief relaxed muscles he hadn't realized were tense. "What if I lost you?" He pulled her close and pulled the towel from her face. He leaned down and claimed her mouth with a kiss. She sighed against him. "Please be careful."

Josie relaxed against him a moment, then pushed away. "To think all I wanted to do was make supper."

He settled at the table and watched her work. "I need to ask you something."

"What?"

"What happened at your tea party?"

"Nothing. Mrs. Allen got offended or upset when I mentioned it would be a great idea if we all got behind a drive for less fortunate children." Josie shrugged. "I think some of the others liked the idea, but they quickly followed her lead. Diane and I may try it on our own."

Art scratched his head. He still couldn't see the problem in that.

"What's wrong?" Josie eyed him as if trying to decipher what weighed him down.

"E.K. placed me on probation today."

Josie covered her mouth. "Why?"

"Something about being unsure I could do my job, and my wife upsetting Mrs. Allen."

She crumpled in front of him. "I am so sorry, Art." She looked crushed. "I only wanted to help. I didn't know how to help, but my mom always has social gatherings like that for the wives of dad's colleagues."

He put a finger on her lips, and she stilled. In the face of her panic, his frustration seemed so petty. He could understand the urge to do something and not getting it quite right. "It's okay. We'll figure this out."

"What will we do?"

"Not panic. I haven't lost my job. I shouldn't, either."

"But why would your Grandfather even let them threaten probation?" Tears streaked Josie's cheeks, giving her the appearance of a child.

"I don't know." He led her to the couch, then pulled her into his embrace.

తా

Footsteps echoed off the stairs, and Josie turned to find Cassandra standing in the doorway.

"Are you okay, Josie?" The girl rushed to her side, fear causing her pupils to dilate.

Josie swiped the tears from her face. "Of course." At the child's dubious look, Josie chucked her under the chin and smiled. "Would you help me with dinner?"

The child bobbed to her feet. "Grilled cheese?"

She looked at Art, who shrugged. "Grilled cheese it is."

After dinner, Cassandra pulled out the checkerboard. "Play a game with me?"

"Absolutely. Hope you're ready to lose." Art struck a pose, shaking both fists in the air like he'd already won the round. Cassandra rolled her eyes.

"Last time, I took all your pieces."

"Luck, that's all it was."

Cassandra shook her head. "I'm happy to show you how real checkers are played."

Josie loved the nine-year-old's poise and spunk. Josie watched her teach Art a thing or two about strategy. This same spirit translated at school where she'd made a couple of friends in addition to Ruth.

After several games where Cassandra trounced him, Josie looked at the clock. "Off to bed, young lady. You still have school in the morning."

Cassandra groaned before leaving to brush her teeth and change.

"She's blossoming."

Warmth flooded Josie. "I think we've hit on what she needs. The freedom to be scared for her family, but also distractions to keep her from living there."

The week passed, and Josie knew she should heed her own advice. She should have had her baby about this time. As the day approached, the grief that had been lulled to sleep reared its ugly head at random times. She'd feel delight watching Cassandra or talking with Art, then be blindsided by sadness and at times anger.

Her arms ached from their emptiness. And she felt alone in that pain. Doris tried to ease it, but Josie didn't want Doris to understand. She needed Art to understand.

Art pulled her next to him on the davenport. "Want to talk about it?"

"It's complex."

"Most things are."

"I miss our baby." A tear trickled down her cheek, and Art brushed it away. "I'm back to wondering. Why did it happen? Why didn't God prevent it?"

"I wish I had answers for you, Josie."

"I just need to know that you miss the baby, too."

Art wrapped her in his arms. "Not the way you do, but I do. I wonder what he would have looked like, but it's different."

Josie nodded.

"Somehow, God will turn it into something good."

"I know. But it's hard to see that right now. Every time I open the Bible, His promises leap off the page. He collects my tears. He promises to turn what the enemy intended for evil to good." She shuddered. "But my arms are still empty."

"Then fill them with Cassandra and me."

Josie longed to be like Joseph. To be able to look at her heartbreak and see how God had turned it into a wonderful thing. Instead, she felt broken and empty. But Art stood next to her. Her promise to him was worth keeping with every fiber of her being.

In sickness and in health. In good times and in bad. She was committed to Art for the rest of her life. And she would live that love.

twenty-two

The vocals of Fred Astaire singing "The Way You Look Tonight" swept into the room from the radio. Quivers ran through Josie as she sat at her vanity. She wanted Art to feel about her the way Lucky Garnett had felt about Penny. . . until he noticed her hair filled with suds.

Her reflection bounced off the mirror. She couldn't find fault with it, but a seriousness filled the edges of her face that hadn't touched her when she'd married Art a year earlier.

One year.

So much had changed. She'd experienced a sadness she'd never known. At times, her breath still caught at the thought of what should have been. But God was God, and she had to trust Him. Trust that He had her best at heart. This year, she'd made the decision to live that trust.

But joy had also filled the year. The joy of knowing the love of a good man. She still didn't know how to describe it other than to thank God for him from a grateful heart.

Art was a gift. She certainly didn't understand him yet. But he balanced her in ways she hadn't expected.

She pinched her cheeks, trying to encourage color to bloom on them. He'd be home in a few minutes, and then they would celebrate their anniversary. Cassandra had already gone down to Scott and Doris's apartment, where she would spend the night.

Art had told Josie to dress up, though he wouldn't tell her where he'd made reservations. The long rose gown in taffeta with its bolero jacket looked like something Ginger Rogers would wear in a formal dance scene. Was that what he had in mind?

The door squeaked. She jumped. That must be Art.

"Honey, I'm home."

Time was up. She pulled the dress over her slip and zipped it as he walked into the room. The sight of her working at the zipper brought a smile to Art's face, the kind of smile that warmed her from the inside out.

"Need any help with that?" The twinkle in his eye conveyed his meaning.

"Oh no. I very much want to see this place where you've got reservations."

"We'll have the best seat in the house."

Something about the way he said it made her a bit nervous. "Am I overdressed?"

Art eyed her up and down. He motioned for her to turn in a circle. She complied, then dipped for a curtsy. "I'd say you're perfect."

His approval brought warmth flooding into her cheeks. How she loved this man.

❧

Josie looked so appealing with the color flooding her face. He loved the way he could make her blush with a look or a whispered comment.

Would she be pleased when she saw what he had planned? He hoped so. The key was to make the evening memorable in every way. A night she would never forget.

His plan should accomplish that. Her thoughts? Well, he'd have to wait and see.

He looked at his watch. "Ready to go?"

Josie plopped at her little table and frowned at him from the mirror. "Do I look ready?"

How to answer that? She always looked good to him. Even when she lay in bed, rumpled from a hard night's sleep, hair plastered to her face, and sleep softening her expression. But how to explain that she was beautiful because she had chosen him?

Laughter filled her eyes. "Give me a few minutes, and I'll be ready." She picked up her brush and made a motion like she would swat him if he didn't leave. He could take a hint.

The sight of her in her gown should have woken him up. Instead, he felt half-asleep and lethargic. Some cold water might do the trick. He turned on the tap in the bathroom and let it run a minute. He scooped water up with both hands and threw it on his face. The blast woke him up but splattered all over his shirt. Not the brightest thing he'd ever done.

He had an excuse, though. It was Friday, and the week had worn him out. The day had taken so many twists and turns at work, he didn't know which way to turn next. E. K. Fine still had clear thoughts on where he wanted the company to go. How it should prepare for the war. He couldn't seem to let go of the company he'd sold. In a few weeks, he'd be gone, but he made life difficult for everyone as he loudly proclaimed his beliefs—beliefs directly opposed to Grandfather's. Art stood in the middle, pulled by both sides of the debate.

A buzzing filled his ears at the thought of the intense argument he'd overheard.

He shook his head. Tonight was not a night to dwell on what happened at work. He could do nothing about that, but he could focus on his bride. She deserved his complete attention.

As she walked out of their room to meet him, he couldn't take his eyes off her. Dressed like that, she deserved his full focus. She'd done something with her hair that made it sweep off her graceful neck. He didn't know what to call it, but he liked it. All she needed was a rose at her ear to be picture perfect. He wanted to smack himself on the forehead. He should have thought of that. What woman didn't like flowers for her anniversary? He certainly couldn't find them in the crisp weather outside. Maybe she wouldn't notice his oversight.

"Shall we?" He offered his arm. He pulled her closer and inhaled the sweet scent of her violet perfume. He could come home to this for the rest of his life. He was blessed among men.

Squeals erupted from the Duncans' apartment as they hopped down the stairs. He loved seeing Cassandra happy, with a smile that lit up her eyes.

"She's happy, isn't she?" Contentment laced Josie's voice.

Art tucked her arm more firmly through his. "She is, thanks to you."

"I'm just grateful God gave me insight." She sighed. "I wish I'd asked sooner."

Wasn't that the case with so much of life? Art would struggle and wrestle with a problem for days, weeks, or even months on his own. Then he'd hit a point where he knew he couldn't fix or solve it on his own. Finally, he'd acknowledge he needed God's help. What a mixed-up way to approach life.

Art helped Josie into the Packard and then raced around to the driver's side. Quiet conversation floated between them, but Josie never asked where he was taking her. She seemed content to let him surprise her.

This had to be perfect.

He so wanted to honor her tonight. Let her know that he knew what this year had been for her. Show her in a way that he couldn't convey with words.

&

Art zipped along streets that Josie was pretty sure she hadn't traveled before. He seemed determined to take her on a grand adventure. In all likelihood, it would rival the journey of their first year.

She settled back against the seat, content to let him have his fun. He fiddled with the radio until he found a song. She scooted closer to him as Tommy Dorsey's band serenaded them with "I'll Be Seeing You."

" 'I'll be looking at the moon, but all I'll see is you,' " Art crooned, making sappy eyes at her.

"Hey, you, get your attention back on the road."

He laughed and pulled to a stop. The engine idled as he leaned over to kiss her. She sank into it, feeling the sparks ignite a warmth that spiraled all the way down to her toes.

With a groan he pulled back, brushing a hand along her jaw with feather strokes. "Have I told you lately how much I love you?"

The words resonated to the core of her being. "I love you more."

"Not possible."

"I think this is a competition we can afford."

His soft chuckle tickled her ear. "Agreed." He leaned away and grabbed the steering wheel. She felt a sudden chill. "Back to the planned activities."

"Spontaneous is good." Did she really purr the words?

Art slipped back into traffic, and after a few more turns, he parked the car. "Here we are."

"Here?" Josie squinted but couldn't see anything she recognized. "Sorry, I have no idea where here is."

He hopped out of the car and then helped her out. "This is the Abbot Observatory."

An observatory?

"Josie, I want to share the stars with you. Here they have telescopes that allow us to see far into space." He led her through some trees to a brick building that looked Greek in its portico style but had a large dome that rose behind the facade.

She bobbled as he helped her up the stone stairs. Once they were inside, she was glad she'd brought her coat. "Why isn't the dome enclosed?"

"The air inside and out needs to be the same temperature, or it distorts the images."

Not only was he handsome, Art remained one of the smartest men she knew.

"What?"

"Amazed by your mental prowess."

He tugged her toward the telescope like a kid leading a parent to the candy counter. "Look through here." He pointed at a piece that stuck out from the telescope.

"All right." She ducked a bit and placed an eye on the piece. What had been pinpricks of light in the night sky evolved into brilliant, pulsing lights.

"Isn't it amazing?"

She nodded, then decided he might not see her in the deepening twilight. "Breathtaking."

"Yes, you are."

Heat flushed her cheeks again, but this time she gratefully accepted the cover of darkness. They explored the night sky until she was too chilled to stay out any longer. Art placed his coat around her shoulders as they walked back to the car.

He turned her toward him. "Josie, I don't say this enough. I know this year has been hard. There are things we would change, but I need you to know that you are the only person I would want to share the experiences with. I'm praying the good always overtakes the bad. But even if it doesn't, I am so glad you chose me."

Twin tears perched on her cheeks, glistening in the moonlight. He dabbed at her tears.

"I love you, Art Wilson."

He linked her arm through his and continued the walk to the car. The Packard came into view, and their pace quickened. He settled her into the car, even helping collect her skirt. He searched her face, and she waited.

Finally, he smiled and leaned in.

With a kiss that left her weak in the knees.

To think she had a lifetime to enjoy those.

That had to make her most blessed of women. And by the look in Art's eye, he agreed.

twenty-three

"Art Wilson. In my office now." E. K. Fine's voice roared across the room.

Art looked up. Charlie gave him a pointed look. Art shrugged. Stan just smirked at him. If he knew what this was about but wasn't telling, Art might have to shake the belligerence out of him regardless of the fifty pounds Stan had on him. Speed and youth had to count for something.

Trailing E.K. to his office, Art kept his eyes and ears open for any information that would be helpful in the meeting.

E.K. barged through his door and headed to his desk. Art stopped as if he'd run into a wall when he entered. Grandfather sat in a chair in front of the desk. Art's spine stiffened, and his senses went on alert.

Would Grandfather allow E.K. to fire him? Art didn't want to think so, but Grandfather had been clear he had high expectations for Art to meet.

"Sit down, Wilson." E.K.'s voice punctured Art's thoughts. Grandfather arched an eyebrow but kept his gaze focused on his steepled fingers.

Only two chairs sat in front of E.K.'s desk. Art sank into the corner of the one opposite Grandfather. Silence settled over the room. Art determined not to fidget but felt like a kid called into the principal's office.

E.K. joined Grandfather in staring at him. Art refused to break the stony silence. They'd called the meeting. They'd have to start it.

E.K. finally cleared his throat. "You're aware I've been concerned about your performance for a while—given you many opportunities to correct deficiencies."

Art clamped his mouth shut until he ground his teeth.

"Mr. Wilson, here, has a proposal he wants to discuss with you. Against my advice, I might add." E.K. stood and huffed out of the room.

Art stared at E.K.'s chair as if the man hadn't left. He could feel Grandfather's gaze. Art turned and met his eyes.

"Well, now." Grandfather leaned forward on the edge of his chair. "Son, I have a proposal for you. I want you to move to Dayton."

"Back to Dayton? Why?" Where was this headed?

"I think you're ready to be brought into the company. Groomed for a position."

Art gawked at him, then spoke with deliberation. "You want me to move my wife again and leave this company?"

Grandfather waved a hand in the air. "As if your wife wouldn't love to move back home. Don't be pigheaded. Come into the business. Learn the ropes. Do well, and you may even become an owner."

Art shook his head. "I can do all that here."

"True, but I'd like a more active hand in developing your career." Grandfather lifted a hand and stopped the refusal that wanted to explode from Art. "I'll leave you to your thoughts. However, I will need an answer by Friday."

"That's tomorrow."

"So it is." Grandfather grabbed his Tyrolean hat and cane from the edge of the desk and walked out of the office.

Words escaped Art. It seemed even his thoughts had abandoned him. He stumbled to his feet, then headed to his office.

Charlie watched him as he grabbed his lunch bag, hat, and coat. "Everything all right?"

Art jangled the change in his pocket as he tried to find his voice. "I'm not sure."

"I'll pray."

Art knew he should respond, but he felt numb, detached from his body. He liked his life well-ordered. It had drawn him to accounting. Work with the numbers long enough, and they made sense. There was a rhythm and pattern to them. One that was often missing when dealing with people.

He didn't know what to think as he walked toward home, the sky dark and heavy above him.

❧

That evening after Cassandra had settled into bed, Josie and Art huddled over the kitchen table. Art held her hand and rubbed his thumb over her fingers. Move back to Dayton? The possibility of moving home excited her. "What do you want to do?"

Art studied her face as if he wanted to search the depths of her soul before answering. "I don't know." He sighed. "Part of me wants to take Grandfather up on his offer. But another part wants to make it on our own. And I know you'd like to move back." His words trailed off.

"What do you want, Art?"

"I don't know."

"If we weren't married and you could do anything in the world?"

"Then I wouldn't work." The hint of tease in his eyes kept her from smacking him.

"I'm serious."

"It doesn't matter, because I am married to the perfect woman." She began to melt inside at his words. "I'm unsure how to interpret Grandfather's offer. Did he buy the company to watch me work? I can think of easier and cheaper ways to do that."

"It seems like a good opportunity."

"I know." He ran his fingers through his hair. "Let's pray."

Josie relaxed. That's what she loved about this man. He was far from perfect, but he knew where to turn. He held her hands and she listened as his rich voice petitioned God for wisdom and direction. Surely it would come.

❧

Soft snow fell from the sky. From the third-floor apartment it looked beautiful. Peaceful. Serene. At street level, it had brought the city to a halt. Art stumbled outside, intending to walk to work, but the drifted snow left the streets and sidewalks impassable. He wasn't disappointed. The snow gave him time to ponder his answer for Grandfather since Art couldn't get to work.

Art sat at the kitchen table, relaxed with a cup of coffee and the paper. He'd let Josie sleep. No need to wake her since they couldn't go anywhere. Maybe once the snow stopped, they could take Cassandra out to romp in it. Maybe sled down the street.

He sipped his coffee, surprised he'd slept so well. Had to be the result of turning his concerns over to God. But in the light of day, he already felt the struggle to pick that burden right back up.

Lord, help me.

Three small words, but they were all he needed. They might be a never-ending mantra through the day, but that was all right.

"Give it up."

The whisper ricocheted through him. Give what up? He cocked his head, heard nothing else, and went back to the paper.

"The bitterness, your pride. Give it to Me."

Art wanted to pretend he didn't understand. He'd made up the voice. The words came from his mind. But he knew it was a directive. One he needed to heed.

The bitterness and pride froze him in place. He didn't like feeling that Grandfather had manipulated him. Yet he knew that wasn't Grandfather's intent. He'd made a good offer that made sense on most fronts. So why wouldn't his grandson jump at the opportunity? Art needed to have his head examined.

No, he needed to obey.

The thought of forgiving, turning his back on his pride—he could hardly stomach it. But he had to. "Does this mean I have to work for the man?"

"Grandfather?" Josie startled him. He hoped his collar hid the heat climbing his neck.

"Yeah."

Josie smiled, and it went straight to his heart. "Probably."

❧

Several weeks later, boxes lined the living-room floor in the corner Josie had envisioned holding the Christmas tree. Even with Cassandra, they'd decided to forgo the decorations while they packed.

Josie stared around the small room, her heart beating erratically. Annabelle had called to say she was on the way. Looking at the piles of household items scattered across the floor, she decided she couldn't feel less prepared. *Father, calm my heart. Help me focus on Cassandra and what's best for her.*

The door opened, and Cassandra and Art stumbled through the door. Cassandra's laugh rang with sweet innocence, and her cheeks were a rosy red kissed by the cold air. Snowflakes clung to her face, probably remnants of a well-aimed snowball. Considering the snow clinging to Art's hair, they'd engaged in a wild snowball fight. Cassandra and Art performed a dance at the door as they knocked trace amounts of snow off shoes and dropped their coats, scarves, and mittens at the door.

"Did you have fun, Cassandra?"

Art didn't look much older than nine himself as he grinned at Josie over Cassandra's head. "Of course she did." He moved as if to tickle her. "She knows she'll be tickle-tortured if she doesn't agree."

Cassandra squealed and turned to run, but Art grabbed her before she could take two steps and threw her over his shoulder. Josie felt a rush of joy as she watched.

"Go get changed, Cassandra. I have a surprise for you when you're dry and warm."

Cassandra perked up. "A letter from home?"

"Maybe." Josie smiled as Cassandra flew to her room and slammed the door. If only that could be motivation every day.

When Annabelle arrived, Cassandra sat covered in a blanket

on the davenport, rereading the letter. Josie expected the letter to rip under the girl's intense gaze.

"Would you like some tea? I also have warm milk for Cassandra's hot chocolate."

"I'm fine." Annabelle eyed the boxes. "So it's final. You've decided to move."

Art had grown excited at the prospect of working for his grandfather. Josie couldn't wait to be back in Dayton near family. But she'd realized through the preparations that Dayton wasn't really home anymore. No, that was wherever Art lived.

"Yes, we'll move in a few days at the school break."

"You're sure that will work for Cassandra?" Annabelle arched an eyebrow.

Josie watched Cassandra read the letter another time. "She'll be fine. She's excited about getting to spend time with our families, too. We can't imagine not having her with us for the duration. We made a promise to her family that we'll keep." Just like she'd made a promise to Art to love him through all circumstances for the rest of her life.

Annabelle nodded, then walked over and joined Cassandra. "Do you mind if I ask you a question?"

Cassandra looked up from her letter and grinned. All was well in her world. "Ma'am."

"Are you willing to move with the Wilsons to Dayton? It will mean a new school and home for you."

"Oh, that's fine. My family will still know where I am. And I don't want to be with anyone else."

Josie hoped the new school would give Cassie a chance to start with a clean slate. And Cassandra and Ruth could stay friends through letters, maybe even visits.

As Annabelle prepared to leave, she seemed settled with the idea. She stopped at the door. "You know how to reach me if there are any problems."

"Yes. Thanks for your assistance." Josie smiled at Annabelle. "You've been such a help with Cassandra."

Annabelle nodded. "It's the part of my job I enjoy the most. Don't forget to keep me posted on how things are going. And I'll still stop by periodically." Annabelle chucked Cassandra under the chin. "You've got a great home, kid."

Cassandra's face-splitting grin agreed. Josie showed Annabelle to the door, then turned to Cassandra. Now if she could just get the child to put down the letter and help with the packing.

◈

Art closed up his briefcase. It somehow latched around the pile of items he'd shoved in it. His desk cleared, Art turned to Charlie. "Thanks for everything."

Stan leaned against his desk, arms crossed. "I know you ain't saying that to me."

Art chuckled. "You weren't so bad. Kept me on my toes."

"Here to serve."

Charlie guffawed. "You've got the better assignment, you know. I'm stuck with this guy."

"You can handle him."

Stan rolled his eyes.

The future stretched in front of Art, largely unknown. Had he made a good decision? He honestly didn't know. All he knew was he'd followed God's leading to the best of his ability. And it was too late to change his mind. His replacement had already started, and the house was packed.

He had a feeling Josie wouldn't be too happy if he suddenly decided they were staying.

Grabbing his briefcase, he shook hands with Charlie and Stan. "Good-bye."

His steps were slow as he walked through Eden Park. It might be December, but he didn't want to rush. No, he wanted to carefully consider everything that had occurred in the past months. There had been joy and sorrow with Josie's pregnancy. The uncertainty with his job. The joy of watching Cassandra gain her footing.

God, You are so good.

Those words cycled through his mind, a meditation of praise.

He walked through the door, surprised to find some order to the chaos. Looked like Josie had at least kicked the boxes to the walls. He might walk through without knocking his shins against a dozen boxes.

Josie hurried to him. "Welcome home."

He pulled her in for a kiss, then deepened it. A year, and he still couldn't fathom God's goodness in entrusting her to him. "Any regrets?"

She eyed him carefully, questions replaced by certainty. "Not one. It's been an adventure, Mr. Wilson. One I plan to enjoy for the rest of my life."

As he stood circling her waist with his arms, he believed her. She was a gift from God, and he would treasure her, too. Their promise was one he'd keep.

A Letter to My Readers

Two years ago I experienced what to-date has been the most excruciating experience of my life. I miscarried after trying for a period of time to get pregnant. To this day, I'm not sure how to answer when people ask how many children we have. I often say three because it's easier, but each time I whisper in my heart, *Our fourth child resides in heaven*. This book grows from that experience and from my deep desire to acknowledge the often unspoken pain of that experience.

Prior to my miscarriage, I was one of those who probably said all the wrong things. I also didn't realize miscarriage occurred in at least 25 percent of recognized pregnancies. To be honest, I had no frame of reference. The pain spun my world on its axis and left me groping for Jesus in the darkness.

The loss from miscarriage—at least for me—is an ongoing pain. Every milestone during pregnancy that was missed. The due date. The anniversary of the loss. The pain is tempered, but present.

One of my friends comforted me most by acknowledging the pain. She said, "When we lose a parent, we lose part of our past. When we lose a spouse, we lose part of our present. But when we lose a child, we lose part of the future."

My prayer for this book is twofold. If you've been blessed to never experience a miscarriage, I hope this will give you a piece of insight so you can better support friends and family in their time of need. And if you've experienced this loss, know I grieve with you and pray God will show you He can turn what the enemy intended for evil into something beautiful. And I pray you catch glimpses of that beauty here and now.

A Letter To Our Readers

Dear Reader:

In order that we might better contribute to your reading enjoyment, we would appreciate your taking a few minutes to respond to the following questions. We welcome your comments and read each form and letter we receive. When completed, please return to the following:

Fiction Editor
Heartsong Presents
PO Box 719
Uhrichsville, Ohio 44683

1. Did you enjoy reading *A Promise Kept* by Cara C. Putman?
   ❑ Very much! I would like to see more books by this author!
   ❑ Moderately. I would have enjoyed it more if

   _____

   _____

   _____

2. Are you a member of **Heartsong Presents**? ❑ Yes ❑ No
   If no, where did you purchase this book? _____

   _____

3. How would you rate, on a scale from 1 (poor) to 5 (superior), the cover design? _____

4. On a scale from 1 (poor) to 10 (superior), please rate the following elements.

   ____ Heroine   ____ Plot
   ____ Hero   ____ Inspirational theme
   ____ Setting   ____ Secondary characters

5. These characters were special because? _____

_____

_____

6. How has this book inspired your life? _____

_____

_____

7. What settings would you like to see covered in future
   Heartsong Presents books? _____

_____

_____

8. What are some inspirational themes you would like to see
   treated in future books? _____

_____

_____

9. Would you be interested in reading other **Heartsong
   Presents** titles?   ❏ Yes   ❏ No

10. Please check your age range:
    ❏ Under 18   ❏ 18-24
    ❏ 25-34   ❏ 35-45
    ❏ 46-55   ❏ Over 55

Name_____

Occupation _____

Address _____

City, State, Zip_____

THE BRIDE
BACKFIRE

Aim to spend plenty of delightful hours reading *The Bride Backfire*, a witty historical romance about two feuding families and a marriage of inconvenience.

Historical, paperback, 288 pages, 5³⁄₁₆" x 8"

_____

Presents

Great Inspirational Romance at a Great Price!

Heartsong Presents books are inspirational romances in contemporary and historical settings, designed to give you an enjoyable, spirit-lifting reading experience. You can choose wonderfully written titles from some of today's best authors like Wanda E. Brunstetter, Mary Connealy, Susan Page Davis, Cathy Marie Hake, Joyce Livingston, and many others.

When ordering quantities less than twelve, above titles are $2.97 each.
Not all titles may be available at time of order.

SEND TO: **Heartsong Presents** Readers' Service
P.O. Box 721, Uhrichsville, Ohio 44683
Please send me the items checked above. I am enclosing $ _____
(please add $4.00 to cover postage per order. OH add 7% tax. WA add 8.5%). Send check or money order, no cash or C.O.D.s, please.
To place a credit card order, call 1-740-922-7280.

NAME _____

ADDRESS _____

CITY/STATE _____ ZIP_____

HPS 7-09